Brander Matthews

The Last Meeting

A story

Brander Matthews

The Last Meeting
A story

ISBN/EAN: 9783744748308

Printed in Europe, USA, Canada, Australia, Japan

Cover: Foto ©Andreas Hilbeck / pixelio.de

More available books at **www.hansebooks.com**

THE LAST MEETING

A STORY

BY

BRANDER MATTHEWS

NEW YORK
CHARLES SCRIBNER'S SONS
1885

CONTENTS.

CONTENTS.

THE LAST MEETING.

CHAPTER I.

FREDERICK OLYPHANT.

THERE are not wanting those willing to abuse the climate of New York, but even the most vindictive of these, after declaring that the cold of winter, the dust of spring and the heat of summer are alike intolerable, finds himself constrained to confess that there is nothing to be said against the few brief weeks of delight which intervene after the hot spells of the African summer and before the cold snaps of the Arctic winter. In these rich and mellow days of the Fall—to use the good old English word often ignorantly miscalled an Americanism—the air is both balmy and bracing ; and the joy of living, the mere animal pleasure of existence, is the portion of every healthy man as he takes his walks abroad. This season is not the mild and enervating Indian summer which may sometimes

follow it after a frost or two ; it is the Fall as it is
seen at its best along the Atlantic coast, after it
has begun to paint the trees and the vines in
ruddy colors which recall the war-paint of the
departed inhabitants of these shores. It is the
season of perfect bodily felicity, when men return
to town, rested and refreshed and ready to buckle
to their winter's work.

On the afternoon of a day toward the end of
October, a day which was a sample of the very
best the clerk of the weather can offer to his
American customers, Mr. Frederick Olyphant,
a young artist, left his studio, in an odd little
building just back of Tenth Street, and, passing
through a dim alley way into the quiet side-
street worn by the feet of three generations of
the artists of New York, turned toward Fifth
Avenue, pausing only to glance at the clock in
the picturesque tower of the Jefferson-Market
Court-house. There was a little tang to the wind
as he walked briskly to the corner and started
up town. He was going to Mrs. Sutton's, who,
that afternoon, was At Home, Tea at Four
O'Clock. It was almost the first tea of the
season. As a rule, Frederick Olyphant disliked
teas, but at Mrs. Sutton's he hoped to meet Miss
Winifred Marshall, with whom he was in love,
and who had promised to marry him.

Frederick Olyphant was as handsome and as
manly a young American as one could have

found in a walk from Central Park to the Battery. There was an air of resolute self-reliance about him. He had clean and clear-cut features; his eyes were deep brown; he wore a full beard trimmed squarely below his chin, and a dark brown mustache curled away from his upper lip. The American and the stranger within his gates are alike ready to praise the beauty of American women, a beauty as lovely in its bloom as it is fragile and fleeting, though it is gaining sturdiness and lasting longer every year, now that American girls live more in the open air and are borrowing the common-sense notions and the healthful habits of English women. But less, indeed, one may say little, is heard about the good looks of American men, although they are almost as much deserving of comment. There is character in the face of an American, and a student of human nature who should stand in Broadway taking notes need complain of no monotony of feature. Now and again he would see a face which might have been painted by one of the great Venetians: there is the same shrewdness, elevation, and mercantile nobility — for New York, like Venice, is a city by the sea, and her merchants are princes. There are young men, too, whose faces are prophetic of the future of the New World—young men whose faces are lighted by hope and strengthened by determination; young men in whose eyes can be seen what the English term Pluck and the Americans call Grit. Many of these young men, eager and energetic, robust in health, and athletic in gait, have their full share of Anglo-Saxon good looks. As handsome as any in vigor and vitality and in manly strength was Frederick Olyphant, walking rapidly and firmly up Fifth Avenue that October afternoon, in the hope of a meeting with Winifred Marshall.

Frederick Olyphant's paternal grandfather had been a Scotchman, but the rest of his ancestry for two hundred years back was New England to the core, sons and daughters of clergymen, given to high thinking and accepting plain living without complaint or protest. Frederick's father was the first of the family to venture forth from New England to New York. This was no doubt due to the transmitted influence of his father, Frederick's grandfather, a Scot abroad, at home anywhere. At the battle of Seven Pines, Major Olyphant was shot through the heart; and when Frederick was twenty-one, a week before he was graduated at the New England College, of which his great-grandfather had been President, his mother died also, and he was left alone in the world to fight his own battles as a man must.

From his father and from his mother Frederick Olyphant inherited what was once known as "a modest competence;" in other words, he had a small, fixed, secure income, quite sufficient to provide him with bread : his butter he must earn himself. This lifting above the necessity of pot-boilers and of hack-work is a great boon to an artist or an author who has the wish always to do his best. Olyphant had early determined to be a painter ; and pictorial art, especially in the beginning, is like literature in that it is a good staff and a bad crutch. To Olyphant his income was a blessing, for it enabled him to study as long as he chose, not merely in the schools of art, but at large among men. He had been born with a certain adventurous restlessness in his blood, and he roamed over the world seeing life. After a hard winter's work in New York he spent a summer in studying the Indians of the Pueblos in New Mexico, and in evolving a new theory of their descent from the Aztecs of Montezuma. The year after, he went with the whaling fleet to the North Pacific. During the war between Russia and Turkey he pushed to the front as the special pictorial correspondent of the *Gotham Gazette*. For three years he did his best at the École des Beaux Arts in Paris.

At all times he delighted in athletic exercises ; he was a mighty swimmer, a skater of grace and endurance and an adroit and skillful fencer. He was a wonderful shot with the rifle and also with the revolver of his native land; his fellow students, in the *atelier* of M. Gérabanel, still tell of his shooting the spots from the five of spades with a revolver, using the sixth shot to drive in the tack by which the card was affixed to the opposite wall of the studio, a distance of twenty metres.

It must not be supposed from this that Frederick Olyphant was a prodigy in any way, a variant on the accepted type of Admirable Crichton. There were many things which he never attempted, although whatever he did, he did well. He had no ear for music, for example, and to earn a king's ransom he could not distinguish 'Yankee Doodle' from 'God save the Queen.' And he had no taste for science; it was with difficulty that he had picked up enough knowledge of figures to master the elements of navigation.

Yet another marked defect in his character was his carelessness as to what he wore. Although he was an artist, he was also a campaigner, a camper-out, and a sailor; and he was triply reckless in his attire. He never knew what he had on. He was wholly free from vanity, and he gave as little thought as possible to his clothes or to his personal appearance. He went always to a good tailor, wherever he might be, and bought clothes of the best quality: then he put them on and wore them without change until they were worn out. It was altogether a matter of chance whether he was the best-dressed man in a room or the worst. He had never quite understood whether his friend Rudolph Vernon, the poet, was serious or not, when he asked Frederick's opinion about a new hat, and wanted to know whether Frederick thought the contour becoming to the poet's head. It was Olyphant's own habit to take the first hat that fitted him comfortably, regardless of its shape. For months he had been wearing a black felt hat, very easy to the head but quite unpresentable. Nor had this carelessness of attire grown on Frederick with his wanderings ; he had always had it ; in his sophomore year at college a new-comer, trying to identify his classmates and to learn their names, referred to Olyphant as "the man who was better dressed than he seemed to be." As the painter walked up Fifth Avenue in the clear sunlight of an October day, there was no fault to be found with his clothes, which were almost new, having been worn only two weeks.

Life is composed of two parts, so the Arab proverb tells us, the past, which is a dream, and the future, which is a wish. As Frederick Olyphant recalled the nearly thirty years of life which were his past, he thought of this proverb. His past had little more of substance than a dream. He had seen much, he had learnt much, he had hoped more,—but he had done little. Now, at last, that the future was a wish indeed, he regretted that he had not begun earlier and that he had not accomplished more. Perhaps it is hardly fair to expect that the man with five

talents shall get quite as good interest on his
having as the man with but two : in time and by
toil the average man may make *cent. per cent.*,
but we must not expect gains in this proportion
from the more highly endowed genius.   Critics
of foremost authority had declared that genius
was scarcely too strong a word to apply to what
they saw in the last two or three pictures which
Frederick Olyphant had painted.   His work was
imaginative in a high degree, though at times it
might seem only fantastic.   His fine allegory
'The End of Time and Space' had been hung
on the line at the Royal Academy the spring
before, while at the same time his 'Spectre of
the Brocken' had taken a second prize at the
Paris Salon.   A German journalist, reviewing the
annual exhibitions of London and Paris, declared
that these two pictures revealed the coming of a
new man, of a new force in art; and that the
Old World should take it as a warning that this
light broke from the New World.   But praise
like this made Frederick Olyphant ashamed of
himself; he knew better than his critics ; all that
he was willing to acknowledge to himself was
that he had learnt the rudiments of his trade.
He knew how to say whatever he had to say ;
but what he might have to express in the future
depended wholly on the essential richness of his
own nature.

The mellow sunshine, which bathed him in

molten gold at every crossing in his quick march to his tryst with the woman he loved, was not brighter than the hopes which filled his heart. He had youth and health and friends ; and there was nothing to which he might not aspire. He had the future before him, and the future is a wish, said the Arab proverb ; and he had already attained the summit of his desire—for she loved him. He marveled at his good fortune and received it as an omen,—for he had inherited from Scotland or from New England a full share of intangible superstition. Knowing his own unworthiness, he wondered how it was that she had chosen him. He accepted her love as the direct gift of heaven, as inexplicable as it was precious. He called up before him her lovely image, and he was lifted up by high and beautiful thoughts. For her sake he would work hard and do his best and put behind him all that was low or mean or paltry.

As he strode resolutely up Murray Hill, he saw an early evening star rising above the horizon and seeming to lead him on, respondent to the exalted hope which filled him. She would be his guiding star in life, as pure and as beautiful as the light which beamed faint and far beyond him. He found himself wondering whether that distant orb were inhabited, and whether any of its inhabitants were one-half as happy as he. Then his gaze dropped, and he took note of the throng which filled the avenue. Men and women and children, on foot and in carriages, going to the Park and coming back from their business; and as he looked at them, they seemed to be happy, most of them, and to be smiling and laughing and to be at ease with the world. But there was none of them with whom he would dream of changing places. There were no ten of them whose combined felicity could equal his. The world was bright and the people he met were smiling, but no one had as good cause for rejoicing as he: and he gave thanks in his heart.

Once at the crest of Murray Hill, Frederick Olyphant slackened his pace, and again gazed up at the star, before he turned into Thirty-sixth Street, where Mrs. Sutton was at home, and where he knew he should find Miss Marshall. His thoughts were raised above earthly things into the glorified ether which lovers only may inhabit. So little was he attending to the men and women about him that it was no wonder that he did not know that he was followed, and that a man, a stranger probably, and from his attire apparently a foreigner, had hung on his footsteps ever since he left his studio. This strange follower kept fifty paces or so in the rear of the artist. As Olyphant turned sharply out of the avenue, the man on his trail hastened forward as though unwilling to let his quarry

slip from his sight. The stately house of Judge
Gillespie, where his only daughter, Mrs. Sutton,
was to dispense tea that afternoon, is but a few
yards from Fifth Avenue, and Frederick Olyphant was mounting its broad steps before the
curious attendant who had dogged him for
nearly half an hour reached the corner. The
young painter stood for a moment before the
door, enjoying the glory of the sinking sun as
it flooded the narrow street with its golden
radiance. The stranger at the corner of the
avenue fell back as Olyphant, recalled to the
affairs of this world, gave a hasty glance up
and down the street, and then rang the bell;
he watched the door open to admit the guest
and then close behind him. He walked slowly
past the house as though questioning whose
it might be. Then he sat himself down on a
doorstep opposite and waited.

CHAPTER II.

WHEN Judge Gillespie's daughter was at boarding-school, whither she had been sent at twelve years of age, shortly after her mother died, Judge Gillespie's house was as comfortable and as commonplace a dwelling as one could find anywhere on either side of Fifth Avenue. But when Judge Gillespie's daughter came back from boarding-school, after having finished her education, and when she came out in society, a great change was wrought in the appearance of the house; it was swept and garnished and its old-fashioned furniture was hidden as far as possible under new-fangled draperies. And when finally, in her second year of society, Miss Gillespie met her fate in the person of Charley Sutton, the only son of Judge Sutton, of San Francisco (who had been the head of the great law-firm of Pixley & Sutton ever since the death of Senator Pixley), she made it a condition of her remaining in New York that she should be allowed to do what she pleased with the house and to spend just as much money

12

in altering, redecorating and furnishing, as she saw fit. Judge Gillespie was pleased with the match ; he saw an eternal fitness in the mating of a daughter of a judge with the son of a judge; but he did not want to lose his only child, and he was prepared to grant her all she asked if in return she would keep house for him as she had ever since she left school. It happened that Mr. Charles Sutton had made up his mind to remove to New York, even before Miss Gillespie had accepted his hand and heart. His sister, Mrs. Eliphalet Duncan, had already married a New Yorker, and he was quite ready and willing to be received into Judge Gillespie's house as a son.

Mrs. Sutton was a determined little woman, as clever as she was pretty, and having her full share of the precocious dignity which is the distinguishing characteristic of a widower's only daughter. She had taste, too,—good taste, and plenty of it, and of the very latest variety. She knew what she wanted; she planned maturely; and when she went to Europe on her bridal trip, she left exact and elaborate instructions behind her. The workmen took possession of Judge Gillespie's old house and tore it limb from limb. He fled to Newport, and even took an autumn trip to Colorado. When Mrs. Sutton returned to New York from her wedding tour, she found a house exactly to her taste; it was the old house no longer; it was made over, altered, redecorated, changed from cellar to attic; and it was a year before Judge Gillespie felt at home in it. From the Beauvais tapestry which hung in the hall, and the quaint wrought-iron railing which protected the staircase of the richest Californian redwood, everything in the house was new and modern and in accordance with the taste of to-morrow.

When Mrs. Sutton was At Home she stood to receive her guests in the front drawing-room, which she had hung and decorated in exact accord with her complexion. As she was a woman of much common sense she had not allowed her advanced taste to run wild; and the front drawing-room looked less like a section of the South Kensington Museum or of a Nuremberg curiosity-shop than do many other front drawing-rooms in which a wandering Briton feels like a John Bull in a china-shop. There was an abundance of rugs, so that unwary man need not slip on the treacherously polished floor. There were many oddly shaped chairs and sofas covered with soft stuffs whereon a man might sit at ease. There were silver lamps with silk shades, and there were candles in sconces high on the walls, casting down a dim religious light upon the attendant vestals who guarded the low altar whereon the fire kept the water boiling and who were frequent in pouring libations of tea.

Mrs. Eliphalet Duncan sat before the little bow-legged table on which the tea-things stood. Mrs. Sutton had another table from which she dispensed cups of white-capped chocolate and dishes of many-colored cakes. Miss Pussy Palmer and Miss Winifred Marshall were " receiving" with Mrs. Sutton—a mysterious function made known to the other guests by the absence of bonnets from the heads of these two young ladies. Mr. Laurence Laughton was talking to Judge Gillespie, while his eyes followed Miss Marshall as she glided about the room in fulfillment of her duties as a deputy-hostess.

"As I understand it," the Judge was saying, judiciously, " the difference between a Tea and a Reception is solely a difference of fare—of provender, if I may venture to use the word."

"I see," answered Laurence Laughton ; " at a Tea, you get tea and cakes, while at a Reception, you expect a square meal."

"Precisely. And the result is that man, being a worshiper of his stomach, shuns Teas, although he is sometimes seen at a Reception."

"Well, I believe you are right," said Laughton. "We are two men here and we feel, both of us, I take it, like a cat in a strange garret."

"*Qu 'allait-il faire dans cette* garret? " quoted the Judge, who prided himself on his accent, and who had once adapted a play from the French.

"A Tea is an excuse for gathering together a lot of women, old and young, so that they can admire each others' gowns to each others' faces," remarked Laughton, "and that being the case, I think your daughter is to be congratulated on the success of her afternoon."

"There are quite a dozen ladies here at this early hour I think," answered the Judge, with paternal pride.

"Two more—I've been counting. And now is the Scripture fulfilled, which said that seven women shall lay hold of one man."

"Why, Uncle Larry, how can you say so?" interrupted Mrs. Sutton, with whom Laurence Laughton was a great favorite. He was a young man of a little more than forty, and he was no relation to her, but he had willingly accepted her, and many another pretty girl, as his niece by brevet.

"Why, shouldn't I say so?" he answered. " Fourteen ladies here and two men only—your father and I. Twice seven are fourteen."

"Don't tell me that," replied Mrs. Sutton, merrily. "I refuse to acknowledge it. I'm like Mrs. Martin there. I never could learn the multiplication table—and, what's more, I don't believe it is so!"

Laughton laughed at this declaration of feminine principle.

"Have a cup of chocolate?" asked the hostess.

"Well, I don't know but that I will sit up and take a little nourishment," answered Uncle Larry, dropping into a low arm-chair by the side of Mrs. Sutton, as Miss Winifred Marshall crossed the room to meet a new-comer. From his new position Laughton was at liberty to follow all Miss Marshall's movements. But his view was at once cut off by Miss Pussy Palmer, who came and stood before him.

"Uncle Larry," said this lively young lady, who was most becomingly dressed in a silver-gray plush velvet, which fitted her lithe little figure to perfection, "I want to know: Is Frederick Olyphant going to be here this afternoon?"

"I want to know, too," was Uncle Larry's guarded answer.

"But is he?" she persisted, seating herself on the arm of a sofa.

"Well, I don't know. I shouldn't wonder if he did come. Why?"

"Because I want to see him *so* badly. Uncle Larry!" ejaculated Miss Pussy, with mysterious vehemence, "can you keep a secret? Well, I'm *desperately* in love with Mr. Olyphant."

"You don't say?" asked Uncle Larry, with amused interest; "and does he return your young affections?"

"I don't know and I don't care. I'm not *serious*, you know. But I think he's just splendid.

2

I only met him for the first time on Sunday, and I think he's the handsomest man I ever saw! Don't you think so ? "

" Well, I don't know how many handsome men you have ever seen," was Uncle Larry's natural response.

" Now I do.   He's lovely.   He has the most beautiful eyes you can imagine.   Why, he's as handsome, in *his* way, as Winifred is in hers. You call her pretty, don't you ? " continued Miss Pussy.

" No; I call her beautiful," said Laughton, seriously.

" That's what I say.   I think she's just the *loveliest* girl I ever saw—and she's as good as she is pretty!   And to think that she is going to throw herself away on a man !   It's perfectly ridiculous ! "

Uncle Larry, with a certain tremulousness of voice, asked, " Is she engaged ? "

"Oh, no; she isn't *engaged*, but she's sure to be some day, you know.   The men are all after her now, and she'll have to take one of them to get rid of the rest."

Miss Palmer was not very observant, and she rattled along without noticing Laughton's little sigh of relief.   He raised his hand to his mouth and stroked and curled his heavy auburn mustache.   His eyes crossed the room, as he raised them again, and rested on the erect figure of Miss Marshall. She was slightly taller than the generality of women, but just then she seemed of an unusual height, for she towered above a little man who had entered the room a minute or two before, and who now stood by her side, rubbing his hands together in a self-deprecatory manner.

"Why, there's Mr. Hobson-Cholmondeley," cried Pussy Palmer as soon as she saw him. "Isn't he sweet? I just *doat* on Englishmen when they're nice. And he isn't half bad, don't you know!"

Uncle Larry smiled at her broad caricature of the English accent.

"Now, you watch," she continued, "and you'll see. He wants to come over here and talk to me. He thinks I'm great fun, though I don't believe he thinks I'm good form, don't you know? But the Duchess will capture him from me,—you see if she doesn't. Sometimes I think the Duchess doesn't quite approve of me." Miss Palmer said this with an innocent expression, as though wondering how it came to pass that anybody could fail to approve of a brightsome little body like herself. She was given to accepting herself as a kitten, whose actions were playful, inconsequent, and harmless.

Mr. Hobson-Cholmondeley, having received a cup of tea from Mrs. Duncan, was slowly making a way for himself through a sudden throng of ladies to where Miss Palmer sat on the arm of the sofa. His path led him near a lady of portly presence and of a dignified manner. This was Mrs. Martin, whom certain of her younger friends chose to call the Duchess of Washington Square. She caught the Englishman's eye as he passed, and he obeyed her imperious glance and meekly took a seat on a stool by her side.

"There now!" said Miss Palmer to Mr. Laughton, "didn't I tell you? She's a *regular* body-snatcher when she gets a-going. Of course, *I* don't care, but it's pretty rough on the stranger to get taken in like that."

Uncle Larry listened with amusement to the innocent prattle of his companion. He wondered how soon she would experience a change of heart, forswear slang and reform her picturesque vocabulary. Just now Miss Pussy was a showy little woman, rather pretty and very young, wearing her bright bronze hair cut short like a boy's. In another year or two, thought the experienced Larry, her tip-tilted nose will be the only reminder of her present pertness, and she will be as quiet and mild in manner as an American girl should be.

Miss Pussy Palmer was the only daughter of a very wealthy man who had lately removed to New York from a little town in the interior of Pennsylvania. Mr. Palmer had once been a bar-keeper, if report may be relied on, and he had struck oil—literally, not figuratively. A three-hundred-barrel well had been discovered on a small farm he had taken for a debt. After exhausting the enjoyments of his native town, and after building and endowing a free public library for its inhabitants, Mr. Palmer had felt the stirrings of social ambition. As Mr. Delancey Jones neatly put it, " Palmer formerly mixed for the best men of Beanville and now he wants to mix with the best men of New York." In this laudable desire he was seconded by his only child, who had just been graduated from a very fashionable school where her lively humor and her sweet temper had made her a great favorite with her classmates. When they came out they promised to help her to come out also. And she had come out with a vengeance, thought Uncle Larry. He wondered why it was that this rattle-brain girl, who was kind-hearted enough, but who had scarcely as yet more than a veneer of " the manners and tone of good society," should be an intimate friend of Winifred Marshall, who was reserved and proud, and whom most people thought cold and haughty.

" Doesn't Winnie look lovely this afternoon ? " asked Pussy, breaking in on Laughton's reflections. " I don't *wonder* she always wears black ; it's so becoming to her. And that big yellow bow suits her style down to the ground."

Laughton felt the justice of this feminine remark. The severity of the rich black silk which fitted Miss Marshall's beautiful figure as no dress fits a woman whose lines are not graceful curves, was relieved by one large and several smaller bows of a deep golden yellow, which accentuated boldly her ivory complexion and her dense black hair. She wore a bunch of yellow roses fastened at her waist.

"She's got a color, too, and that's *always* becoming to her. Don't you think she looks a little restless?"

"I had not remarked it," answered Uncle Larry, considering Miss Marshall even more intently than before. Perhaps she felt the force of his gaze, for she looked up and smiled at him brightly.

"Of course, *you* wouldn't see anything," said Miss Pussy, "you're a *man*. But I know her, and I guess she's getting tired of waiting for her young man."

Laurence Laughton found himself wishing that the reform of Miss Palmer's language might take place even sooner than he had anticipated. "Her young man?" he repeated, coldly.

"You know whom I mean."

"Indeed, I do not."

"Then you are blind—or else you must be in love yourself, Uncle Larry. Why, *everybody* has seen how devoted Frederick Olyphant has been to her all summer. I heard of it in a dozen letters. Girls were writing to me about it all the time."

Laughton wished that girls had found some more profitable employment for their leisure.

"He just *worships* the ground she walks on. I don't suppose she cares for him, you know, but he can't keep his eyes off her. That's what I'm told. And I'll punish him for being late to-day—that is, if he comes at all. I'll waylay him, and get up a flirtation with him in spite of his teeth. You see if I don't!" Despite the freedom of her vocabulary there was no trace or taint of vulgarity in Pussy Palmer's manner: her brilliant smile made a man ready to forgive linguistic enormities greater than hers.

At this moment there was a change of position. Mrs. Sutton called Miss Marshall to take her place at the chocolate table. Once ensconced behind this counter, the lady in charge could serve only one customer at a time, for the little table was almost in a corner, and access on one side was cut off by a projecting Japanese cabinet. Scarcely had Winifred taken her seat, before Frederick Olyphant entered the room by the door nearly opposite to her. Their eyes met at once, and a smile lighted both faces.

"There he is now," cried Pussy Palmer. "Uncle Larry, you go and get me a cup of chocolate and a cake. I haven't had a *single* bite yet, and I am as hungry as a cannibal in

Lent." She gave this order with a child-like imperiousness which was one of her most fascinating little ways.

As Laurence Laughton left her to obey this command, she waylaid Frederick Olyphant. Laughton noticed that, as Miss Marshall was preparing the cup of chocolate, her color heightened and then fled, leaving her with an unwonted paleness. When he returned to Miss Pussy, he found that she had installed Olyphant in his place.

" You must not make me sit down now," Olyphant was saying; " I am famished, I want a cup of chocolate, or I shall expire of inanition."

" You shall have it at once," responded the lively Pussy, taking the cup from Laurence's hand and putting it in Olyphant's, despite his ineffectual protest. " Here's my cup. It's leap-year, and so it is a girl's *privilege* to wait on a man. Uncle Larry, will you please get me another cup ? "

Laughton smiled at the pitiful expression on Olyphant's face, and departed again on his quest. He remarked a defiant excitement in Winifred Marshall's manner, and he caught a fierce gleam from her large, black eyes.

" You are not well this afternoon," he ventured to remark, with ill-concealed interest.

" Oh, yes, I am," she answered, as her tea-rose complexion grew richer under his gaze.

"You look excited. I think you are feverish," he urged; "let me take you out of this crowd."

"Thank you, Uncle Larry," she said, with a pleasant laugh, "but I'm having too good a time here to want to go just yet. Here's Pussy's second cup!"

"It's her first really, for she gave the other to Fred," explained Laurence, inadvertently.

"I did not know he liked chocolate," said Winifred, quickly. "He told me once that he couldn't drink it!"

"Perhaps Miss Palmer has cast a spell over him, and he must perforce partake of the potion she proffers him."

And after this alliterative speech, Uncle Larry took the second cup to Pussy, who was in violent combat with the painter on the subject of art, about which she, of course, knew less than nothing, and about which he had deep convictions.

"Uncle Larry," she cried, as Laughton approached, "you must come to my rescue. I've been telling Mr. Olyphant that I'm just *mad* about art; and yet he won't give me any art news."

Laughton had a keen recollection of a visit to the gallery of pictures of which Miss Palmer's father was the proud possessor, and he recalled only two or three works of real value amid a mob of paintings which looked as though they might, in some earlier stage of existence, have been chromos.   He smiled gently, and asked,

" What do you want to know ? "

" I'd like to know what he's painting now."

" I'll tell you that," said Olyphant, " if you promise not to ask any questions about it."

" I promise."

" It's to be called 'The Sharpness of Death,' " said the painter.

" Oh, I think that's a *horrid* name !" cried Pussy, pretending to shiver; " can't you change it ? "

CHAPTER III.

MISS PALMER had relieved Laurence Laughton of the second cup of chocolate, and he felt himself at liberty to pass on, abandoning the unwilling Olyphant to the tender mercies of Pussy. On his way across the room to rejoin Winifred Marshall, he was hailed by Mrs. Martin:

" Colonel Laughton—I mean, Mr. Laughton ! " Laurence Laughton had come out of four years of hard fighting in the Army of the Potomac with the title of Colonel, U. S. V.—a title he made haste to lay aside as soon as he was mustered out. He had retained the erect bearing of the soldier, and he had always the gentleness of manner which generally characterizes the man of war. Yet this gentleness failed to prevent his annoyance whenever his military rank was flaunted in the face of strangers. Mrs. Martin knew this, but she was a great respecter of titles, and it was hard to forbear the use of his. She seemed so sorry for this slip, however, that he relaxed the frown with which he had approached her.

" I'm so glad to see you here this afternoon,"
she said ; " I thought you did not condescend to
teas."

" Well, I don't know that I do," Laughton
answered.

" But you must, or you would not have come
to-day," continued Her Grace. " I was saying to
Winifred Marshall, the last time we met you at a
reception, that you were getting to be quite a
society man."

" I'm afraid I do not really deserve the compliment," he replied, with only a dim suspicion of a
smile at the corner of his lips.

" You know Mr. Hobson-Cholmondeley, don't
you ? " she asked.

" Oh, yes, I know Uncle Larry," interrupted Mr.
Hobson-Cholmondeley, who was sitting by the side
of the Duchess. " There is a club called The
Full Score, and we are all going to dine at
Uncle Larry's house to-night."

" Mr. Hobson-Cholmondeley," said Mrs. Martin, "seems to take an interest in Miss Palmer—"

" Such a lively girl ! " interrupted Mr. Hobson-
Cholmondeley.

" But she is not good style," said Mrs. Martin,
as though passing sentence.

Laurence Laughton joined Winifred Marshall
again, and lost the rest of the conversation between
the Duchess and her English friend. Perhaps it
was as well that he did not hear it.

Mr. Hobson-Cholmondeley was a nice little man, with a pair of little mutton-chop whiskers, and a little trick of rubbing his hands together gently. He had a very quiet manner and a very deep voice, which seemed wholly out of place in the mouth of such an unassuming little fellow. He was the younger son of a younger son of an English peer. The title was old and the head of the house was poor. He had to support himself as best he could ; he was an artist, not without talent ; he was a critic, with much minute knowledge of obscure points in the history of art ; he was a poet, in his leisure moments ; he had written a novel or two ; and he had had a classical play damned. There was a rumor that he had once contributed to the *Saturday Review* a social essay on the ' Idiosyncrasies of Ratiocination ' : and there was no doubt that he had once written to the *Times*, for the letter was extant : it was a protest against the conduct of a policeman at Charing Cross. He had lately inherited a small but sufficient income from an aunt whom he had never seen. In his politics he was an advanced radical ; and, although delighted with America, he deprecated the spirit of conservatism, which he declared to be the chief characteristic of the United States. It was understood that he was at work on a volume of ' Notes on America ' ; and he had lectured before the Nineteenth Century Club on the ' British Peerage.'

Naturally the Duchess took a great fancy to Mr. Hobson-Cholmondeley and piloted him through the shallows of New York society. She had a broad tolerance for all political heresies; it was only lapses from the conventionalities of polite society that she visited with swift and fatal punishment. Mrs. Martin was known to her familiars as the Duchess of Washington Square, because she was as prominent in society as might be the most exalted peeress in her own right, and because she dwelt in Washington Square, which has now regained the fashion it had lost for a score of years. She had a majesty of demeanor and an amplitude of raiment which was wont to strike awe into the breasts of all beholders; but she was ever gracious, as became a lady whose social superiority did not need to be asserted; and to an Englishman, the younger son of a younger son of a peer, she was doubly gracious, as became a lady who had once lived in Philadelphia, and whose great-grandfather had been a Tory during the Revolution. She was very hospitable; she was an admirable hostess; and her Sunday evenings in Lent were delightful gatherings. It is true that purists had declared the company " rather mixed"; and when Uncle Larry once vouched for a lady on the ground that he had met her at Mrs. Martin's, Delancey Jones said, scornfully, "You might as well say you had met her in

Central Park." It was Delancey Jones, too, who, in allusion to Mrs. Martin's fondness for bringing out new people, had wickedly called her a " social incubator "—a gibe for which the kind-hearted Duchess had not readily forgiven him, although she had been accustomed formerly to refer to him as " Dear Jones."

" Miss Pussy Palmer is not as beautiful as Miss Marshall," said Mr. Hobson-Cholmondeley to the Duchess after Uncle Larry had left them ; "*pas tout à fait*, but she is a most fascinating little woman."

" I trust you will not allow her to fascinate you," remarked the Duchess, with dignity.

" Oh, dear, no. But she is a type ; I like to study her. She's so different to our English girls, you know."

" She is very different from most American girls, I am happy to believe. Look at Winifred now : see her perfect manners."

" I'm delighted to look at Miss Marshall, I'm sure. She is by way of being a very handsome girl," retorted Mr. Hobson-Cholmondeley, "but she doesn't look happy, and Miss Palmer is so very jolly, don't you know."

" So you do not think that Winifred is happy ? " asked the Duchess.

" I knew she was not happy directly I saw her," declared Mr. Hobson-Cholmondeley, with more perspicuity than the Duchess had credited

him with. Keener observers than the jolly little
Englishman had seen traces of a permanent sorrow in Winifred Marshall's usually sad expression. It was rarely that her eyes lighted or that
her countenance glowed with pleasure, although
she had been known not unfrequently to affect a
gaiety as boisterous as was possible to so reserved a nature. When she was off her guard
and the set smile faded from her lips and her
features could be seen in betraying repose, even
a dull man might mark the veil of haunting
melancholy which clouded her face. As the
Duchess and Mr. Hobson-Cholmondeley looked
at her across the room, they saw her glance
about with an air of bold defiance, at variance
with her usual gentle demeanor. She had just
given Uncle Larry a cup of chocolate, heaped
high with frothing cream, and, as he stirred it in
silence for a moment, she was surveying the still
thronging guests. Although she forebore resolutely to look long in that direction, her eyes kept
returning, involuntarily to the sofa where Frederick Olyphant sat by the side of Pussy Palmer.

"She's a stunning fine girl!" said Mr. Hobson-
Cholmondeley; "it's an awful pity she shouldn't
be happy."

"She has a noble character, and she has led a
sad life," responded Mrs. Martin.

"Dear me; you don't say so?" queried the
Englishman; "has she had a cruel step-mother?"

" How did you know that ? " asked the Duchess, in surprise.

"I didn't know it at all. I guessed it, you know. We Britishers can guess sometimes, like you Yankees do."

" If you have never heard her story, I suppose I ought to tell you—"

" I shall be delighted, I'm sure."

" Because," continued Mrs. Martin, speaking out of the fullness of years of social experience, " if you do not know it, you might accidentally make some awkward allusion to it and—"

" And that would be very unpleasant indeed," assented Mr. Hobson-Cholmondeley, who had a slight difficulty in pronouncing the letter R ; he did not flatten it into W as do some of his countrymen, nor could he give it any roll at all. In general he avoided the difficulty by omitting the troublesome consonant. In the present instance what he really said was that it " would be ve'y unpleasant indeed."

But the ear of the Duchess of Washington Square was not attuned to the seizing of orthoepic subtleties, and if in no others, in matters of pronunciation at least she accepted the will for the deed.

" It is not a very easy story to tell. However, I'll do it as well as I can, if I can only remember all the names." Here the worthy Mrs. Martin did herself injustice, for upon all points of descent

3

and intermarriage her memory was unimpeach-
able. She knew and remembered the exact date
of everybody's birth—although she kept her
own carefully concealed—and she could give
you the exact date of everybody's death. Dear
Jones had said once that the Duchess had a
"tombstone memory."

"I have lent you my ears," said the attentive
little Englishman.

"I suppose I must begin at the very beginning.
Did you ever hear of Captain Thaxter Randolph?"

"Wasn't he a traveler or some fellow of that
sort?" asked Mr. Hobson-Cholmondeley.

"That's the man. He was an Arctic explorer.
At least he was an army officer. I can remember
when he was a professor at West Point;" and
here a vague smile flitted across Mrs. Martin's
face as though she had recalled a tender memory.
"And, of course, he went with his State. When
the war broke out he was a Virginian, you know,
one of the real old Randolphs. So when the
war was over he had nothing to do. He did not
care to go to Egypt or to Brazil, as so many of
the best people in the South did. He got his
friends together and they raised the money for
an expedition to discover the open polar sea."

"I remember now," said Mr. Hobson-Cholmondeley; "very interesting, I'm sure."

"During the war, Captain Randolph had

married Miss Winifred Southgate, who had been ordered out of Washington and sent through the lines, because she was a rebel spy and was constantly sending news to the enemy. She used to flirt with the Union officers in the most outrageous way, and sometimes they would let out a military secret or two, and she would send this valuable information at once to the rebel chiefs."

" Clever girl," remarked the listener.

" But not at all the sort of woman you would like to marry."

" Oh, dear, no ! " was the quick response.

" Once in Richmond," continued the Duchess, " Miss Southgate flirted with the Rebel officers just as she had flirted with the Union officers in Washington."

" She didn't play spy on both sides, did she ? " asked Mr. Hobson-Cholmondeley. " That would be a mean trick."

" Oh, no. She was too good a rebel to do that. With the Southern officer she flirted and carried on because she liked it. And one day Thaxter Randolph married her."

" Poor chap," remarked the Englishman, with kindly feeling for a fellow-man in trouble.

" I suppose she fascinated him. They say she was very pretty, and the men were always after her. I remember hearing Judge Gillespie once describe her as ' a tall, handsome woman with an aggressive bust and a deficiency in her code of defensive morality.' "

" Very clever, indeed," laughed Mr. Hobson-Cholmondeley ; " brings the woman before you at once—like a picture. *Apropos*, I wish it would bring her before us.   I think I should like to see her."

" If you will only be patient, I will tell you what became of her—all in good time," said the Duchess, with a slight severity of tone, for she did not like interruptions when she was engaged in a narrative.

" *Mille pardons*," promptly apologized the interrupter.

Mrs. Martin graciously resumed :

" Thaxter Randolph had married Winifred Southgate, in 1863, and he had time to find her out by 1865 ; and sometimes I have been inclined to suspect that one reason why he went up to the North Pole was to get away from his wife. She had wealthy relatives here in New York, and he left her with them ; and scarcely was his ship out of sight of Sandy Hook before she began flirting again. The man she saw most of was Hildreth Marshall, the famous architect, you know. He was no fit company for any married woman—certainly not in those days. He had studied in Paris for years, and I suppose it was there that he had learnt all his wickedness. When he first came back he had so bad a reputation that all the women wanted to ask him to dinner just to see if he was as wicked as people said. He was a handsome man, and he had delightful manners. When he first made the acquaintance of Mrs. Randolph he was building the Church of Saint Mary Magdalen, you know, in Twenty-seventh Street, —the one with the lovely stained glass windows, illustrating the text, ' Let him who is without sin amongst you cast the first stone.' They say that when he went up in the morning to oversee the work, he was sure to find Mrs. Randolph walking down as he was walking up, and that they met in this way almost every day. That was the winter when Captain Randolph was locked in the ice near Cape Despair."

" It was 'a cold day' for Captain Randolph, as you say here," remarked Mr. Hobson-Cholmondeley, with a smile which betrayed his consciousness of having said a good thing.

" You must have picked up that slang from Pussy Palmer," retorted Mrs. Martin.

" Is it slang ? " answered the Englishman, innocently ; " I thought it was an Americanism."

" Before Captain Randolph returned to civilization, late the next summer, Mr. Marshall had gone to France. But somebody must have told the Captain the gossip about his wife, for one day in September, nearly twenty years ago, he left his house and went to a hotel and blew his brains out."

" Dear me ! " was the listener's sole tribute to this tragic reminiscence.

" In a few weeks Mrs. Randolph sailed for Europe. People said she had gone to meet Hildreth Marshall, but it happened that he returned to New York ten days or two weeks after her departure. In her hurry to remove herself away from New York with its painful associations—and they must have been painful even to her—she left her little child behind her."

" Did she have a child, then ? " asked Mr. Hobson-Cholmondeley, in astonishment.

" Winifred over there, in front of you; the Winifred, now called Miss Marshall, is the only daughter of Mrs. Randolph," answered the Duchess, enjoying his surprise.

" Then I do not wonder she is not happy, But—"

" Listen, and you shall hear all. When Hildreth Marshall learnt that Captain Randolph had committed suicide and that Mrs. Randolph had gone to Europe, leaving the baby Winifred behind, he sought the child out and took a great fancy to it. When Mrs. Randolph died he adopted Winifred."

" I was wondering how it was her name was Marshall. And so Mrs. Randolph is dead ? "

" Her end was almost as terrible as her husband's. She lived in Paris until the siege, involved in all sorts of intrigues, political and personal. She had a great liking for politics, and she was always scheming and plotting. During the siege of Paris, while the French government was at Bordeaux, she came over here on some sort of a secret mission. She was a very pretty woman then ; but she was not received at all, although the men gave her dinners at Delmonico's. Hildreth Marshall avoided her, and went out West for two months to be out of her reach. She petted Winifred, with a great show of affection, and she dressed her up in the latest French fashions. Then, suddenly, without notice, she went away again, as unexpectedly as she had come. She had taken the steamer *Ville de Nice* for Bordeaux, where her political friends were, but she never arrived. The *Ville de Nice* was caught in a great gale in the Bay of Biscay and sprang a leak. They had to run the ship ashore and to land in the small boats. The surf, which was very high, upset the boat Mrs. Randolph was in. All the other passengers were saved ; but Mrs. Randolph sank to the bottom at once, dragged down by the weight of twenty thousand dollars in gold which she had concealed about her."

"That *is* an odd way to die," commented Mr. Hobson-Cholmondeley. "There's a Frenchman's book about 'Les Morts Bizarres,' you know, but there isn't anything even in that queerer than your story. Did they ever get the gold ?"

"When the storm went down, they found the body with the gold on it."

"How very singular!"

"As soon as the mother was out of the way, Hildreth Marshall adopted Winifred. I have heard that Mrs. Randolph left the child to him by will. He was devoted to Winifred, and no father could have been fonder; and she worshiped him. She had never really had a mother to love her, and, of course, she could not help loving Hildreth Marshall. He was ready to make any sacrifice for her. Judge Gillespie says that Marshall would not have married at all, except to give his adopted daughter the benefit of his wife's care."

"Dangerous experiment, I fancy," ventured the Englishman.

"It was a very dangerous experiment, indeed, and it turned out very badly, as it happened. Mrs. Marshall never liked Winifred, and although she did not actually ill-treat her, the child was never happy. I used to have the poor little thing at my house as often as I could, but her step-mother hated to let her come to me. I suppose she was afraid that Winifred might complain; but she never said a word: she was staunch and loyal and kept her sorrows to herself. I think it was the knowledge that he had made a mistake which saddened Hildreth Marshall's death-bed. He left Winifred half his fortune and he appointed Judge Gillespie her guardian. He died only two years ago—so Winifred has not gone into society at all until this year. I believe Mrs. Sutton is going to give her a Delmonico ball just before Lent."

Mr. Hobson-Cholmondeley scarcely heard these last sentences. He was looking at Miss Winifred Marshall, with kindly interest in his eyes. Then he turned to Mrs. Martin, and asked:

" Do you suppose she knows the whole wretched story, as you have told it to me?"

" I hope not, sincerely," answered the Duchess. "She has had enough sadness and sorrow without that. She has lost her mother and her father; she has had an adopted step-mother to tyrannize over her; and her childhood and youth have been far from happy."

" I suppose, now, that all these things affect her chances?" asked the English visitor.

" Her chances?" queried the Duchess, doubtfully.

" Of getting married, don't you know?"

" Oh," said Mrs. Martin, "I think not; Winifred has a great many admirers. There's Mr. Olyphant, the artist, and Colonel Laughton— he's not very young, perhaps, but it would be an excellent match."

While Mrs. Martin and Mr. Hobson-Cholmondeley were talking about her, Miss Winifred

Marshall arose from the little seat behind the chocolate-table and left the room, smiling at them pleasantly as she passed their corner near the door. For a few minutes already the throng of ladies had begun to lessen, and there were signs of an early ending of the social ceremony.

"I must be going; really I must!" said Mr. Hobson-Cholmondeley, holding out his hand to the Duchess, and giving hers a hearty shake. "I have to thank you for a very pleasant after-noon, and I shall try to remember the interesting tales you have told me."

Then he made his way to Mrs. Sutton, who was now presiding over the tea-table.

"Can't I have another cup of tea?" he asked, plaintively, rubbing his hands together gently.

"Why, certainly," answered Mrs. Sutton, pre-paring the beverage. "It's so kind of you to like it, though it *is* genuine English breakfast tea."

In England, Mr. Hobson-Cholmondeley had never heard of "English breakfast tea," and he wondered what it might be, not knowing that it was an American invention. Although he was not gifted with even a man's small share of tact, he did not express his wonder. Instead, he pro-duced a little speech, which had served him before. He took the cup which Mrs. Sutton handed him, and he sipped a little, and said:

"Delicious, simply delicious. Your tea, Mrs.

Sutton, is like the waters of the fountain of Trevi, in Rome, you know, because when a fellow has once tasted it, he is bound to return again for some more."

" *Qui a bu, boira*," remarked Judge Gillespie, who was standing just behind his daughter.

Before Mr. Hobson-Cholmondeley could cap the Judge's quotation, he was seized by Miss Pussy Palmer, who had been doing her best to get up a mild flirtation with Frederick Olyphant, but who abandoned the painter the instant that the pleasant little Englishman escaped from the Duchess.

CHAPTER IV.

JUDGE GILLESPIE was an easy-going man, moving through life along the line of least resistance; for the sake of peace, he had allowed his daughter to do whatever she pleased, when once he had consented to her reconstruction of his comfortable house. There was only one relic of the earlier state of the house which he strove to save. This was a verandah, in the rear of the dining-room, and overlooking the spacious grass plot which extended behind the house to the next street. On this verandah, in the pleasant mornings and evenings of spring and fall, the Judge liked to smoke his cigar while he read the newspaper. But his daughter was remorseless, and in the reconstruction of the house, the verandah had made way for a retreat of her own devising, a compromise between a bay-window and a conservatory. This extension beyond the dining-room was rather too large to be called a bay-window, and it was decidedly too small to be dignified with the name of a conservatory. It was a very pretty little greenery,

44

and, although its glass and iron afforded few architectural opportunities, Mrs. Sutton had contrived to give it a Japanese effect, by the use of a hanging lantern or two, and a few transparent shades of Japanese manufacture, and by the moulding and painting of the slight iron uprights in imitation of the bamboo. As Dear Jones had said when Mrs. Sutton rashly asked his opinion, it was quite as Japanese as any one could expect—in New York ; and it harmonized so well with the dining-room,—which was fitted with a mantel and wainscoting of solid English oak, the spoil of an Elizabethan manor-house. Mrs. Sutton may have seen the latent sarcasm in Dear Jones's praise ; but it did not lessen her liking for the Bower, as she called it, and she closed her eyes resolutely to any insufficiency or incongruity. The Bower had a southern exposure, and even in mid-winter it was arrayed with plants in full bloom. From the dining-room it was divided only by the delicate tracery of a teak-wood screen, the involute interstices of which were veiled and obscured by the polished leaves of a luxuriant ivy, twining to the ceiling and almost masking the narrow entrance. This natural screen, thus beautifully parting the Bower from the rest of the world, made it a favorite resort of those of Mrs. Sutton's young friends who had tender confidences to exchange. Uncle Larry had called it one day the " Lover's

Retreat"; and he declared that three of the most important engagements of the season had been made within its shallow recesses.

When Miss Pussy Palmer released Mr. Frederick Olyphant, he looked about the drawing-room to find Winifred Marshall, but she was not visible. The guests were thinning out rapidly, and locomotion was no longer difficult. He passed through the music-room into the dining-room but she was not there. He wondered if she could have gone to her room without giving him a chance to speak with her. He did not think she could be so cruel, as she knew he had come to Mrs. Sutton's tea only that he might have a few words with her. He had walked the length of the house without finding her, until he stood before the screen, which parted the dining-room from the Bower. Then, with a sudden stride, he brushed through the pendent ends of ivy and stood beside the woman he loved.

" Winifred ! "

" Fred ! "

There was a slight suggestion of coldness in her greeting, contrasting sharply with the warmth of his.

" Why didn't you come to my rescue," he asked, " and release me from that chatterbox? "

Winifred moved slightly, so that he had to take away the arm he had thrown around her waist as he kissed her when he entered the Bower.

"I thought you were enjoying your conversation with the chatterbox, as you call her."

"A chatterbox she is!" said Frederick.

"She is a friend of mine, remember," replied Winifred. "And she is a very pretty girl, too—I've heard you say so. And you have called her amusing; so I never thought of interrupting you."

"Winifred!" said Olyphant, gravely.

"Well?" she answered, with slight petulance.

"You are not jealous, are you?"

"Jealous?—Of Pussy? No, indeed!" she replied, indignantly.

"What else am I to think?"

"You may think what you please, but you have no right to make such absurd accusations. Jealous, why, Fred, I am astonished at you!"

"Come, Winifred, we must not quarrel, I—I should never forgive myself if I said an unkind word to you!"

"Then why do you do it?"

"Did I?"

"You did."

"Then won't you forgive me?"

"I don't see why I should."

"But you will, dear, won't you?" he urged.

"I don't know," was her hesitating answer.

"Yes, you do. You know you are going to forgive me,—why should I have to persuade you?"

" But I like to be persuaded," and she smiled.
He kissed her again.

" Then I am forgiven ? " he asked.

" Just this once," she replied, " but you must never do it again."

Fred laughed lightly. " I do not know now what it is I have done," he said, " but I promise never to do it again."

" Now, tell me what Pussy was talking about to you all that time."

" I was talking about you," answered Fred. " I really don't know what she was talking about."

" Perhaps she was satisfied to look at you. I heard her say once that you were the handsomest man she had ever seen."

" I'm sorry I cannot return the compliment. She's a pretty girl, of course, but—"

" So ; you confess it ? " cried Winifred, archly.

" I can't help seeing it. She's pretty enough as girls go—"

" As girls go ! hear him ! " said Winifred, laughing, with a slight undercurrent of excitement; " I cannot allow my sex to be spoken of disrespectfully, even by you."

" If they were all like you, Winifred, I could not help being respectful to them all," answered her lover, earnestly.

" Well, Pussy is pretty enough as girls go; now, go on ! "

"But how can I think of her," he asked, "when I have seen you!"

"Fred!"

"I hope I have taste enough," continued the artist, with feeling, "not to confuse merely trivial prettiness with a royal beauty like yours."

A rich blush mantled Winifred's cheek as he fixed his ardent eyes on hers. She hesitated. "You do not," she said, "you do not really think I'm pretty?" And she gave him a little side-glance as enchanting as possible.

"Look through my eyes into my heart," was his answer, "and you will contradict yourself!"

"Then you do love me a little?" she asked.

"Love you? I cannot do anything else. Have I not told you so a hundred times?"

"Perhaps—but I like to hear it again."

"And it delights me to repeat it," said the lover. "I love you with all my heart and soul. It is happiness to be with you, to see you, to think of you. Why, Winifred, you are more to me than all the world—more than this world and the next!"

"Hush, Fred; you must not say that!"

"But I have said it, and I mean it!"

"I would rather you did not mean it," she said, gently laying her hand on his arm. We must try and help one another to do our duty in this world that we may deserve the next."

"Winifred, you are my Providence, my fortune,

4

my fate!" He lifted her hand from his arm and kissed it. As he lowered it from his lips, his eyes fell on the ring on her finger. His expression changed and a cloud passed over his face.

"Where did you get that ring?" he asked.

"It was my mother's—indeed, it is almost the only relic of her I have."

"How is it that I have never seen it before?"

"It has been locked up in the Judge's safe for the summer, and I got it out only this morning. It is an unusually fine opal, and my mother had it on when she died," said Winifred, with a softening voice.

"That is a sad memory to have attached to an unlucky stone," remarked Olyphant.

"Do you believe in the opal's bringing bad luck? Are you superstitious?" she asked, in wonder.

"Have you just found out that fault of mine?" he queried in return. "I must confess I am half inclined to believe in amulets and in omens. You know I am a mystic and I have traveled in the East, where it is sacrilege to doubt signs and wonders."

She had taken the ring from her finger and held it in her hand doubtfully. "It seems impossible that anything as beautiful as this should bring ill-fortune."

He gazed at the ring for a moment, as though peering with a subtler insight into its mysterious heart. "Does not its iridescence," he asked at last, "remind you of the dying embers of hope?"

"How strangely you said that!" murmured Winifred; "I believe you really are superstitious and you half convert me."

"Let me wear the ring for you," he said, suddenly.

"And give you my bad luck?" she answered, clenching her hand lest he might take the stone.

"From you to me nothing is of ill omen. I can take the bad luck away from you, but it will not bring me any ill-fortune. Let me have it," and he took her unwilling hand.

"I should like you to wear a ring of mine, Fred, but not this one."

"Why not?"

"Because—because it is an opal."

"But this opal is the ring of yours I want; I shall be satisfied with no other, and, if you must know, I need a ring to wear now, for I cannot find my cat's-eye."

"Isn't it very unlucky to lose a cat's-eye?" she asked, with a little hesitation.

. "So they say," was his answer. "But if so, the loss has done its evil work for to-day, I trust, and the bad spirit is exorcised."

"Have you had bad news to-day?" she queried at once, with sudden interest.

"Give me the ring and I will tell you."

She allowed him to open her hand and to

take the opal which he put on the little finger of his left hand. Then he kissed her palm where the ring had lain, and he said :

". The bad luck I have had to-day is passed, I hope. It was to be kept from you for an hour by a chatterbox. Isn't that the worst fate which can befall me, now I know that you love me ? "

" Oh, Fred ! "

" Couldn't you see I wanted to be by your side ? " he continued.

" Then why didn't you come ? " she retorted, archly.

" How could I get away ? I was in the toils of the chatterbox."

" Remember that she is a friend of mine."

" Then I wish your friends all knew that we were engaged. When I got away from Pussy Palmer, I was in mortal fear lest the Duchess might seize me."

" She's a dear old lady."

" If she had kept me from you for another hour, I should have been ready to denounce her as a worldly and self-seeking old woman."

" She has been a kind friend to me, Fred."

" Then I will forgive her all she may say about me in the future. And it is not her fault if she detains me. She doesn't know that I belong to you."

" Nobody knows it."

" Why should not everybody know it ? I'd

like to cry it aloud from the house-top, I'm so proud of you!"

A sudden sensitiveness sent its tremor through Winifred. "But I do not want to be cried aloud from the house-top; my love for you is the tenderest secret of my heart. I shrink from having it talked over at clubs and street-corners."

"Why should you care about idle gossip?" he asked.

"I am over-sensitive, I suppose," she said, with a little shiver of disgust.

"It is six weeks since you let me tell you that I loved you, and in these six short weeks I have had only stolen meetings with you, as though in my love for you there was something to be ashamed of; and yet you know that nothing in the future, no success in life, no honors, no glory, can ever make me proud if I am not proud now, because you love me!"

Winifred said nothing; she looked at him with love in her eyes.

"I fear I am fanciful," she said, with some little excitement in her manner. "I cannot bear ·to share the secret of my love with any one and every one. As long as we alone know it, we belong to each other and the world is none the wiser."

"But unless you want to have a secret marriage after a secret engagement, people must know it, sooner or later," persisted Frederick.

"I have told you what I think of a fashionable wedding in New York," she answered, vehemently. "I think it is disgusting. On the most important day of my life, I don't want to be a staring-stock for everybody. Sooner than be married at Grace Church with six bridesmaids, eight ushers, little girls strewing flowers and the wedding march from 'Lohengrin,' I believe I'd elope! I think I would rather be married by the mayor, or even by an alderman. I could not make such a degrading show of myself. I should feel as though they were selling tickets at the door!" And Winifred ended this reckless speech with a sharp satiric laugh which betrayed not a little nervous strain.

"Surely, you will not ask me to consent to a private marriage?" questioned Frederick.

"A private wedding is just what I want," she answered.

"But not a secret wedding?"

"Oh, no; people must know some day, I suppose. But there is no need to make a spectacle of ourselves when we get married, is there?"

"Don't you want a few friends to be present?"

"I have very few friends, indeed. I could fill a house with my acquaintances and I can take all my friends out driving in one carriage. There are not a dozen persons I care to have invited to the wedding. And I don't see why anything need be said about the engagement until—until—"

"Until we know when we are to be married,"
added Frederick, coming to her rescue. "Have
it as you please, my darling. Your will is law
to me. I will keep my tongue tied and say
nothing."

" It is best to let the engagement be a secret yet
a while," she went on. "Perhaps we are not
sure of one another. How do I know you will
not tire of me ? "

"Winifred!" cried Frederick, with ardor, as he
threw his arm about her and turned her face up
to his.

" Well," she said, gazing up into his eyes, with
confidence, as though satisfied on that score.
" How do you know I haven't made a mistake
in trying to love you ? "

" Do not torture me," he said, gently, yet firmly.
"We must not trifle with our love ; it is too
sacred to jest with, if it is too sacred to be talked
about. And if you have told nobody of our engagement, I will tell nobody until you bid me."

" I have told nobody at all—that is to say—
well, I have *told* nobody—" and here Winifred
paused in momentary confusion.

" Well ? "

"I know I ought not to have done it, Fred,
but I did. I was writing to Baby Van Renssellaer, you know—she married Delancey Jones last
spring. She was really a friend of mine, and
she is away on her wedding trip, and so I

thought she would understand me, and I let it slip out."

" You wrote her that we were engaged ? "

" Yes ; was it very wrong ? "

" It was not wrong at all," answered Frederick, with a suspicion of coldness in his voice ; " you are at liberty to tell whom you please."

" But I did not mean to tell even her," cried Winifred, impetuously.

" But you did tell her."

" Why shouldn't I if I wanted ? " asked Winifred, with a return of her earlier excitement. " You just said I could tell whom I pleased."

" Certainly," answered Fred. " The matter is not worth talking about."

" Then why do you keep on talking about it ? "

If Frederick Olyphant had let the question drop then and there, he would have spared himself many hours of self-reproach. But he could not let it rest. He was logical, masculine, and persistent. So he went on :

" Because I wondered why you would not let me tell Uncle Larry, if you meant to tell Mrs. Jones ? "

" But I did not *mean* to tell her at all ! " replied Winifred, with equal persistence. " It slipped out by accident. You can tell Uncle Larry, if you like,—you can take as many men into your confidence as you please ! "

" You must not speak sharply to me, Wini-

fred," he said, gently, suppressing his feeling.
" I am wrong, of course.   Whatever you do is
right."

She drew herself up with dignity, and asked
him, in a voice which trembled in spite of her
efforts to control it, " Do you think it is manly to
vent your sarcasm on the woman you pretend to
love ? "

" Pretend to love ? " cried Fred, forgetting
himself. " You do not mean to say that you
doubt my love for you ? "

" If you loved me, you would not treat me in
this outrageous way ! "

Frederick Olyphant was a just man ; he was
just to himself as to others, and he could not
listen to this charge calmly.

" Perhaps I had better relieve you of the insult of my presence ? " he asked, fiercely.

" Perhaps you had ! " she replied, mastered by
the excitement which had been gaining on her
all the afternoon. " And perhaps you had better refrain from calling again !" she added, as he
moved toward the door of the Bower.

" Winifred ! " he cried, in a last appeal, as he
stood with hand on the ivy-clad screen.

" Mr. Olyphant," was her icy retort. They
stood for a moment facing each other in silence.
Before either of them spoke again, Mrs. Sutton
came into the dining-room and discovered them.

" Why, is that you, Mr. Olyphant ? " she cried.

" Yes," he answered, with what composure he could muster; " Miss Marshall and I have been having a chat here in the Bower."

" It's a lovely spot for a quiet flirtation, isn't it ? " said Mrs. Sutton, as he withdrew from the door in the screen to allow her to enter the Bower.

He waited a few seconds, hoping for a kind word from Winifred. But she stood silent and haughty. He turned to go at last.

" Won't you stay to dinner with us ? " asked Mrs. Sutton. " The Judge is always glad of a chance to chat with you,—and if he has to go out early, Winifred and I will try to amuse you."

" I am sorry that I have an engagement," was his answer, " or I would remain with pleasure. As it is, I fear I have trespassed here too long. I have to thank you for my afternoon."

" I am very glad you have amused yourself," said Mrs. Sutton, graciously ; and then, without a word from Winifred, Olyphant left the house.

It is a pity that the story of lovers' quarrels need ever be told, for it is a miserable story, at best. Winifred Marshall and Frederick Olyphant loved each other with the deep passion of strong and noble natures ; they had been betrothed for six weeks ; and this was the first time they had not found themselves of one mind. It was their first misunderstanding, and it turned on a trifle that neither of them could declare with exactness.

Each felt a sense of injustice and injury; and each was sustained by false pride. Perhaps if Mrs. Sutton had not intervened when she did, just as Olyphant was about to go, he might have stayed his feet or Winifred might have recalled him. But it was not to be. Theirs was a true love, and its course was not smooth. They quarreled, as lovers will; they parted, as lovers before them have done a many times; and the pain and smart of the parting were bitter and hard to bear.

It was about the edge of dusk when Frederick Olyphant left Mrs. Sutton's and walked hastily to Fifth Avenue, with his head high in the air and a keen pang in his heart. The sun had set and a dim haze clouded the streets. The afternoon had been bright and joyous, but the evening was gray and dreary. When Olyphant arrived at the corner of Fifth Avenue, he gave no thought to the star he had hailed as he ascended Murray Hill, and he cast no glance behind him; he turned sharply and strode down the avenue at a sturdy pace. Had any one been trying to follow, he must needs have moved briskly.

But as Frederick Olyphant left Winifred Marshall farther and farther behind him his pace slackened and his stride relaxed. He walked on in deep thought, with his head down and his hands behind him. He felt as though the light had gone out of his life. The streets, which had

been gay as he passed them on his way to meet
her, seemed now, as he came back from seeing
her, dull and dismal. Even the people had
changed in their manner toward him ; before he
had remarked the many fine-looking men and
the crowds of smiling pretty girls ; now he saw
only withered old hags and ungainly ruffians,
who scowled as he strode by them. As he crossed
Madison Square, there was a chill sprinkle of
rain, and he wondered why he should feel the
cold keenly, after the hardening of two campaigns
with the Russian troops. And so, with changing
thoughts and an aching heart, he plodded on his
dismal way, until at last he rang the bell at
Laurence Laughton's door.

At that moment Winifred Marshall had locked
herself in her own room, after sending word that
she had too severe a headache to sit at dinner.
She lay on her bed, weeping hot tears of self-
reproach.

CHAPTER V.

THE FULL SCORE.

MR. LAURENCE LAUGHTON was a universal favorite, especially with dumb animals, with little children and with young ladies. He could not always at once recognize every pretty girl who greeted him as "Uncle Larry." He was a young man of a little more than forty years of age, a young man still, for all his two-score years and more. No one had ever ventured to call him old or even to think of him as elderly, for he always felt young and mingled with young people; and he thought of himself always as young, and while a woman is as old as she looks, a man is as old as he feels. There was as yet no suspicion of baldness on his head, thickly covered with rich auburn hair, with a graceful tendency to curl. There was no hint of grey as yet in the long tawny mustache which drooped over his lip. His bearing was always erect and military. He was not an ill-favored man, even if one did not regard the intelligence and the kindliness which shone from his face.

Larry Laughton was a man of varied accomplishments; he told a story excellently, with an abundance of dry and unaffected humor; he played a fairly good game of billiards; he rode as became a colonel of cavalry; and Miss Pussy Palmer had been heard to declare that he danced divinely, although when he was enticed to a ball he was more likely than not to sit out the cotillion in a quiet corner with a clever woman. He was the sole executor of a wealthy aunt, and the management of this estate gave him sufficient occupation and a sufficient income for his modest wants. He was fond of traveling, and he ran across the ocean nearly every summer, ready for a trip to Spain or to Sweden, and yet content to dwell quietly in London, where he had numberless friends. During the Russo-Turkish war he had spent several months in the field with Frederick Olyphant, going afterward through the Holy Land and up the Nile, taking notes by the way. These impressions he had been persuaded to publish and his 'Myrrh, Aloes and Cassia,' aided by Olyphant's illustrations, had been one of the milder successes of the year in which they were published. He owned his house in New York in Fifth Avenue, not far from Union Square; and he kept it open for his friends. And of friends he had a many. As Frederick Olyphant once said, "Uncle Larry had a gift for friendship." He was prompt with a kind word for all strugglers ; and during the past twenty years many a young author and artist had found in Larry an uncle who did not demand security for what he might lend. He had a faculty of divining silent grief; and in ministering to it his touch was as delicate as his insight was keen. He was a man to whom his friends turned for consolation whenever trouble fell on them. He was a man, also, without whom no festivity was complete.

It was Laughton who had suggested the founding of The Full Score, a little club which was to dine with him on the evening of the day when Mrs. Sutton gave her tea. Half-a-dozen of his friends happening to be returning to New York on the same ocean-steamer one September, he had proposed that they form a dining-club to be limited to twenty and to dine together three times a year,—in the fall and in the spring in New York, and in the early summer in London. Like Larry himself, most of the members of The Full Score were unattached bachelors, artists, authors, actors and musicians, almost as frequent in their visits to London during the season as he was. Although all the members were Americans, except the latest, Mr. Hobson-Cholmondeley, some of them were sure to be in London every year, enough of them, in fact, to make a dinner-party exceeding the canonical limit of nine. The name of the club, The Full Score,

indicated the extent of its membership and contained a suggestion also of its artistic characteristics. It was now four or five years old, and
its three dinners a year had been partaken of
regularly with an abundance of good-talk and a
strengthening of the bonds of good-fellowship.
In London the club dined about here and there,
trying one restaurant after another, from Green-
wich to Richmond. In New York The Full
Score were always the guests of Laurence Laughton, who gave them two dinners a year, one
toward the end of October, the other about the
beginning of April.

As Frederick Olyphant walked straight from
Mrs. Sutton's, he was the first arrival at Uncle
Larry's. He was as familiar in the house as
though he were a younger brother of its owner—
and rarely indeed does a closer and a deeper
friendship unite two men than that which bound
together Laurence Laughton and Frederick
Olyphant : they had faced death side by side.
Therefore, when the door was opened by the
faithful Bridget, who had been in Uncle Larry's
employ for fifteen years and more, Fred passed
her with a smile and a query as to where Mr.
Laughton might be found.

" He's been home this half-hour, sir, and he's
in his room now."

Olyphant hung up his hat in the hall ; and he
went up stairs, where he was received with much

pantomimic enthusiasm by Bundle o' Rags, Laughton's favorite little terrier.

" You are the first to come," said Uncle Larry, as Olyphant entered the dressing-room where the host was vigorously brushing his hair. " Have a cocktail while we are waiting ? "

" I don't want a drink now," answered his friend, in a spiritless voice ; " and I doubt if I can do honor to your dinner."

" What has made you so down-in-the-mouth ? " asked Larry, turning sharply around and looking at Olyphant with interest.

" I'm good-for-nothing to-night ; dull and miserable."

" You are not ill, are you ? "

" I'm sick at heart ; don't question me about the reason, for I mustn't tell you. And I have an oppression in my head, too."

" In your head?—there's nothing in that, you know," said Larry, encouragingly,—" if there is not anything else."

" There's really nothing more, I suppose ; and yet I feel, somehow, as though something was going to happen ; I feel much as I felt in Plevna when you nursed me through that attack."

" Well, I don't know that you have any call to have another of those attacks now," said Uncle Larry, cheerfully. " Brace up, man, and don't borrow trouble ; most anybody will lend it to you quick enough, but you have to pay

5

such heavy interest on the loan that it's not a profitable transaction."

"Oh, I'm all right! Don't worry about me." And Olyphant made a resolute effort to shake off the gloom which had enfolded him. "What time is the dinner?"

"Seven, as usual."

"And how many are there to be?"

"Fourteen this time — unless Dear Jones manages to get here."

"Is he back?" asked Olyphant.

"I suppose so," answered Larry. "The *City of Constantinople* arrived about noon, and they were to come on her."

"Then he'll be here, of course."

"Well, I don't know," said Uncle Larry; "when a man arrives home from his wedding-trip he is not very likely to leave his bride and come to a stag dinner."

"Do you think Mrs. Delancey Jones would object, then?"

"Perhaps not; but I hardly expect him. In time I suppose we shall all be tied to some pretty woman's apron strings—you and I and all of us."

Olyphant gave Larry a sharp look to see if there was any ulterior significance in these words.

"When The Full Score were organized as a club, we were all bachelors, and now the girls are carrying us into camp every year. Charley

Sutton and Eliphalet Duncan and Rudolph Vernon and Dear Jones, one after another, have joined the married majority."

"Friend after friend departs," quoted Fred, with an effort at cheerfulness.

"But they come back after a while," retorted Larry, "and knock at the gate again." Just then there was a ring at the door. "There's one of them, now—the married men are always the first to come. Even if Dear Jones fails us, we can count on all the rest of them."

"And there's Poor Bob White,—he is sure to be here—and he was the first of us to get married," remarked Fred, with a sudden recurrence of his melancholy, humorously heightened by the lugubrious strains of a hand-organ just under the window.

Larry Laughton put on his coat and they went down to greet the arriving guests. In the hall they met Rudolph Vernon, the poet, and his intimate friend, J. Warren Payn, the young composer. Rudolph Vernon was always precise in his attire; there was no touch of poetic frenzy in his garb; he had been heard to say that he "didn't see why a poet shouldn't dress like a gentleman." He had brought back from Paris a long blue-black, cloak-overcoat, buttoning high in the throat, draped with an ample cape, making him look, as Larry said promptly, "like a younger son of one of the Pilgrim Fathers."

Mr. J. Warren Payn, who had set to music several of Vernon's songs, was the organist of two Episcopalian churches, for one of which he composed a full choral service every Easter; his spare time he spent on the score of a comic opera, of which he had high hopes, and fragments of which were frequently sung for him by the obliging ladies and gentlemen of his church choir.

"Well, Payn," asked Uncle Larry; "how are you getting on with 'Montezuma'?" The composer's friend knew that 'Montezuma' was the title of the comic opera.

"First rate!" answered the composer. "I have finished scoring the second act and I have just had a capital idea for a topical song in the third—good for four encores every night."

There came another ring at the bell, and Mr. Charles Sutton and his brother-in-law, Mr. Eliphalet Duncan, arrived together. They were followed shortly by Mr. Robert White, who wrote for the *Gotham Gazette* under the name of 'Poor Bob White.' Then came Mr. Hobson-Cholmondeley, rubbing his hands together gently.

"I'm not late, am I?" he asked, in his deep voice. "I should be so sorry to have kept you waiting."

In a few minutes Laughton's rooms began to fill up. As is often the case in bachelors' houses, the front parlor, devoid of feminine attraction, was abandoned, and the men clustered naturally in the more masculine library. Uncle Larry's house was three rooms deep; the parlor fronted the avenue, the dining-room was in the rear, and the library with its huge folding-doors connected the two. Like most middle rooms in New York houses, the library had no windows; and in the daytime it received its light wholly from the dining-room on one side and from the parlor on the other. But at night, lamps over against the mirror, and a bright fire of crackling hickory, made it as warm and pleasant a retreat as one could wish in winter. The two longer walls of the library were lined with bookcases, broken on one side by the fire-place, a structural part of the book-case it divided. On the other side, in one of the sections of the book-case, was a little door, concealed by a curtain and leading into the hall; although this door was the only means of entrance directly into the library, it was very rarely used, as most people passed through the parlor or the dining-room.

High over the bookcases and close under the ceiling, was ranged Uncle Larry's collection of death-masks, a collection in which he took great delight, which had cost him an infinity of pains, and which was absolutely without equal in the United States. There from the top of the wall, staring down at the chance visitor, with their sightless eyes, were the faces of the great Dante, of Goethe and of Lincoln, wise above other men, with their features now relaxed beyond recognition almost, and fixed here forever in death. There were strange juxtapositions among those blank white visages, and men who reviled each other when they lived were now cheek-by-jowl, now that they were dead. There are contrasts in death as in life ; and a man might moralize for a month upon the plaster-casts which hung over the bookcases in Uncle Larry's library.

"What a charming house you have here," said Mr. Hobson-Cholmondeley, to the host as he entered the library; "really, I had no idea." Then he raised his eyes, and saw the long line of white faces, silent and staring. "Dear me!" he ejaculated, his voice dropping even lower with surprise. "Pray, what are these?"

"That's a collection of death-masks I have been getting together during the last twenty years," Uncle Larry answered.

"Fancy now!" said Mr. Hobson-Cholmondeley. "You Americans have such queer tastes."

"We air a remarkable people," declared Charley Sutton, talking through his nose, "and you Britishers ought to know it."

"Really you do use some of the most extraordinary words," continued Mr. Hobson-Cholmondeley. "I went down to the city this morning—"

"To the city?" asked Sutton, in surprise.

" Yes, to Wall Street, you know," explained the Englishman. "And there was a great excitement there; it appears they have just struck a bonanza; is that the word?"

" Bonanza—that's right enough."

" A bonanza in the Baby Mine, and they say it is bound to be a big boom."

Mr. Sutton was a Californian by birth, and gossip about mines was as the breath of his nostrils: "A bonanza in the Baby Mine?" he cried, with great interest. " I don't believe it, I guess it is salted."

" Salted?" queried Mr. Hobson-Cholmondeley, not understanding, " *Qu' est-ce que c'est que ça?*"

" I mean, that it was a put up job, that they found only the silver they had put there themselves," explained Mr. Sutton.

" Dear me," exclaimed the Englishman, " do they do things like that?"

" Don't they? But I don't care; I've got a lot of stock in the Baby Mine and this find will let me out."

" Only fancy," remarked Mr. Hobson-Cholmondeley, dubiously, rubbing his hands together in wonder as to whether the Californian were chaffing him or not.

In the meanwhile, other members of The Full Score had arrived. There was a young doctor of twenty-five, who was fortunately as bald as a billiard ball, and who therefore passed for thirty-five, to the material increase of the confidence of his patients and his own practice. There was a young sculptor, who had recently finished the fifth Soldier's Memorial he had been commissioned to execute within three years, and who was beginning to wish that he might have a chance to commemorate the victories which peace hath as well as war. There was a young painter, who had given up ambitious historical subjects, to devote himself to household decoration, wall-papers and stained-glass, and who was rapidly making both a name and a fortune.

The guests gathered in the library, with little groups overflowing into the parlor. Rudolph Vernon was holding forth to Warren Payn and Robert White against the absurdities of modern society. "I agree with Lord Byron," he declared, vehemently,

"'Society is now one polished horde,
    Formed of two mighty tribes, the Bores, and Bored.'"

"There's another Byronic quotation more pertinent just now," interrupted White; "I am waiting for—

'That all-softening, overpowering knell,
    The tocsin of the soul—the dinner bell.'"

"And you shall have it as soon as the last man comes," declared Uncle Larry, who had chanced to hear the quotation.

"We are all here now," responded White, "except Harry Brackett, and he asked me to have him excused, as he might be very late or even kept away altogether."

" What's the matter?" asked Larry.

" The opera company arrived on the *City of Constantinople* this afternoon, and he has to interview them all for the *Gotham Gazette.*"

"What, all of them?" enquired the host. "Then, we need wait no longer. Let us pass into the banqueting hall!"

The folding-doors were thrown open, and the ample table in the dining-room stood revealed. Laughton's own household was not equal to a dinner fit to set before The Full Score, for Larry, although of simple tastes himself, and ready to rough it on occasion, was not unfriendly to the good things of this life; and, moreover, he had a due and proper respect for the fine art of dining. He was fond of having his friends about him, and more than once had her grace, the Duchess of Washington Square, matronized lively little parties of young people, dining with their Uncle Larry before going to the play, or supping with him after feasting on the horrors of tragedy. He always suited his fare to his company; and he set before The Full Score a very different bill of fare from that discussed by the young ladies whom Mrs. Martin had under her wing. The *entrées* and the ices were Larry's chief care when he had young people of both sexes about his board ; while for a stag-dinner he gave his attention mainly to the game and to the wines. Although the dinner was vicariously supplied, the cook and the waiters had been to the house a dozen times before, and everything was served with perfect precision. Laughton was an excellent host, unassuming and all-seeing, never putting himself forward and yet never forgetting that he was the host, and that the host should hold himself responsible for the comfort and enjoyment of the guests.

As The Full Score placed themselves about the round table, every man choosing his own seat, Mr. Hobson-Cholmondeley broke the silence by remarking, in a deep voice, " *Tiens, tiens*, we are only thirteen."

" Thirteen ?" repeated Frederick Olyphant, turning a little paler.

" Thirteen precisely," responded the little Englishman ; " I counted directly we came in."

" There's luck in odd numbers, said Rory O'More." This was the solace offered by Charley Sutton.

"And it is Friday, too!" added Rudolph Vernon.

" Thirteen ?" repeated Olyphant, counting hastily in the hope that there had been an error. " If it is, I suppose it cannot be helped."

" It doesn't make you uncomfortable, does

it?" asked Robert White, who sat at Olyphant's right hand, as Olyphant sat at Larry's.

"Why not?" responded Frederick, trying to turn it off with a laugh. "I accept all superstitions as premonitions of future scientific discovery."

"We are thirteen now, but it is only until Harry Brackett arrives," urged Larry, "and he is sure to be here before we break up. So this thirteen doesn't count!"

"Perhaps we ought to do as the old Gauls are said to have done," suggested White; "whenever they found themselves thirteen they drew lots and killed one of their number on the spot, for fear that the unlucky combination should cause somebody's death in the course of a twelve month."

"Perhaps" hazarded Rudolph Vernon, "we might send for a fourteenth—"

"To fill this living sonnet, as I suppose you poets would call it," interrupted Sutton, looking at Vernon.

"I know a man who lives around the corner," continued Vernon, "and you all know him; he's a fellow poet. If I propose him as a member I know you will all give him a unanimous vote—in the negative."

"You must mean Tapp?" said Sutton.

"Of course," added Eliphalet Duncan.

"Tapp it is," Vernon responded. "Do you want him as a member of this club?"

There was a sudden and tumultuous shout of " No!" from everybody else, a shout which bore testimony to the extreme unpopularity of Mr. S. Clozen Tapp, a young poet not without ability, but best known for his lofty self-appreciation and for his over-sensitiveness to criticism.

" Gentlemen," began Eliphalet Duncan, " I draw your attention to this terrapin; it is divine!"

" Liph worships his stomach," was the comment of his brother-in-law.

" And pampers his god with burnt offerings," added White.

" The undevout gastronomer is mad," Uncle Larry declared.

Mr. Robert White noticed that Frederick Olyphant had turned all his glasses upside down. " You are not a cold-water man, are you," he asked, in surprise. " Do you stick to croton *extra sec?*"

" Why not?" Fred demanded.

" That's another of your left-handed ideas," rejoined White. " You drink cold water, and you object to thirteen at table."

" Look not on the wine when it is red," quoted Fred, with a smile.

" I have always considered that a most misleading text," said Uncle Larry, intervening, " for it drives a man to white wines, which are not half as wholesome as the red."

Thus led into a gentle debate, Frederick Olyphant struggled vigorously with the gloom which oppressed him, and also with the purely physical discomfort about which he had spoken to Uncle Larry on his arrival. He took his share in the paradoxical discussions of Shakspere and the musical glasses, which form the staple of talk at a gathering of enthusiastic young men, most of whom had strong artistic inclinations, even when they were not by profession workers in one art or another.

Toward the end of the dinner the conversation took a turn which forced Olyphant to the front. One of the lawyers was making fun of Mr. S. Clozen Tapp's last novel, 'A Young Lady from Long Island,' which White irreverently called 'The Girl from Gowanus.' He was especially satirical on the introduction of a duel into an American novel in this last quarter of the nineteenth century.

" That's all very well," retorted Rudolph Vernon, " and I do not want to say a word in defence of Tapp's book, but the disappearance of the duel gave as great a blow to romantic fiction as it did to polite manners ! "

" The duel hasn't altogether disappeared." declared Charley Sutton ; " in New Centreville, once, I saw two men fight with bowie-knives. Out West many a man dies with his boots on."

" Fancy ! " said Mr. Hobson-Cholmondeley,

making mental notes of a new fact in American civilization.

"I don't call butchery with bowie-knives a duel," retorted the poet, indignantly. "A duel is an affair of honor, fought out with rapier and dagger—"

"Pistols and coffee," interrupted White.

"The duel," continued Vernon, not noticing this interjection, "got its artistic value from the fact that it was often the final station of an elaborate scheme of revenge. But now, nobody dare use revenge as the basis of a story."

"Good subject for an old-fashioned essay for the *Arctic Monthly*," Olyphant suggested: "'On the Disappearance of Revenge as an Element of Modern Fiction.'"

"I think that revenge has gone out in literature," White remarked, "because it has gone out in life. Nowadays a man doesn't sit up nights to hate another man; he cuts him in the avenue on Sunday, and thanks God he is rid of a knave!"

"Well, I don't know," Uncle Larry interposed. "Out West, as Charley Sutton said, men still take speedy vengeance on their enemies. Out West there is still a survival of the ordeal by battle, and disputes are settled by the arbitrament of the bowie-knife."

"But, Uncle Larry," urged White, "that is quick temper, not slow revenge."

" Poor Bob is right this time," said Eliphalet Duncan ; " revenge is played out."

" It may be played out in the West, Liph," declared Frederick Olyphant, " but in the East it is alive and kicking."

" In Corsica, now," suggested Mr. Hobson-Cholmondeley.

" In Corsica, and still farther East, in the Levant, generally," continued Olyphant. " Wherever the Turk and the Greek have met, there are long hatreds yet, and the slow revenge of malignity is as possible now as it was in the Middle Ages in Italy."

" Do you think so ? " asked Mr. Hobson-Cholmondeley.

" I know it ! In London and in New York a man's life may be safe enough from revenge ; we English-speakers are a law-abiding race in the main, and our law is served out to us with justice, for the most part. But in the Orient revenge is a motive more potent than love."

" How very interesting ! " said Mr. Hobson-Cholmondeley.

Frederick Olyphant had warmed to his work as he spoke, and his wonted reserve was broken through.

" Why, if I were to die to-night," he went on, " if I were to be killed suddenly and mysteriously, even here in New York, I should know that my death lay at the door of one man, a man

whom I have met only twice, but who warned
me that the third meeting would be fatal."

" *Tiens, tiens,*" said Mr. Hobson-Cholmondeley.

"You mean Constantine Vollonides, I suppose?" asked Larry. "The man with the Black
Heart."

" That's the man," returned Olyphant, " Constantine Vollonides."

" You ought to tell them the whole story,
Fred," remarked Uncle Larry; " how you saved
the man's life the first time you met him; how
you spared his life the second time; and how he
then warned you that the third meeting would
be the last meeting."

" I say, Fred, this is not fair," declared White;
" you might have let me interview you for the
Gotham Gazette : it would have been copied in
half the papers in the country."

Fred smiled and answered, " I did tell Harry
Brackett something about it once, and he worked
it up in one of his out-of-town letters."

" Then you must tell us now," cried Charley
Sutton. " The truth, the whole truth and nothing but the truth ! "

Olyphant shook his head.

" But you must; we insist," said Bob White.

Fred remained silent. He had a sudden
return of the oppression, physical and moral,
from which he had been suffering since he

parted from Winifred Marshall. He felt that it would be impossible for him to tell the story.

"Uncle Larry, to you we appeal," White cried; "you are the Lord of the Revels and the Keeper of the Green Seals, and you must unlock the lips of the great silent man."

"Come, Fred," Uncle Larry began, when Olyphant interrupted him:

"Let me suggest as a compromise that you make Uncle Larry tell the story."

"I accept the amendment," said Charley Sutton, promptly; "Gentlemen of The Full Score, those of you who are in favor of hearing from Mr. Laurence Laughton the strange story of Constantine Vollonides, the man with the Black Heart, will please say Aye!"

There was a thunderous chorus of Ayes.

"But I protest," began Uncle Larry.

"Contrary minded, No," continued Sutton. "The motion seems to be carried,—it is carried. Uncle Larry has the floor."

"Uncle Larry has no use for the floor at this early hour of the evening," responded the host. "But I am willing to tell the tale, if Fred won't."

"Fred won't," said Olyphant. "And if you will excuse me, Larry, I'll go into the library and write a note."

"You mustn't go, Fred," urged Robert White. "How do we know what kind of a yarn Larry will spin us, if you are not here to see fair play."

6

" Perhaps I shall get back before he comes to the sticking-point," replied Olyphant, as he rose from the table and passed into the library. He was perfectly at home in Laughton's house, and knew just where to help himself to paper and pen and ink. He took his seat before the large desk-table in the centre of the library, in front of the blazing fire of crackling hickory logs, and began to write a letter to Winifred Marshall.

CHAPTER VI.

THE MAN WITH THE BLACK HEART.

"NOW, Uncle Larry, tell us the tale of the man with the Black Heart. No doubt it is gruesome and weird, not to say marvelous and melodramatic," said Poor Bob White. "Nothing extenuate nor aught set down in malice, but give us the cold truth, *la verité frappée*, as we say in French."

"Well, I don't know," responded Uncle Larry, "just how to tell you the story or exactly where to begin."

"Begin at the beginning, of course," suggested Rudolph Vernon; "strike the lead at the out-croppings and get right down to pay-gravel, as Charley Sutton would say."

"Invoke the Muse," retorted the young Californian; "perhaps she will help you out, and even if she doesn't, you fill out ten lines or so, which is worth consideration when editors pay for poetry at column-rates."

"You see, the difficulty is," Uncle Larry continued, "that I wasn't present at the first meeting between Fred and Vollonides. I can bear witness to the second, because I was there all the while; but as to the first, my evidence is not evidence at all, is only hearsay. I had liefer Fred told you himself; still, if he won't, I must do the best I can to give you at least the pith of the story."

"Tell the tale as best you can," remarked White, encouragingly, as he lighted another cigarette.

"Well," said Uncle Larry, "as you all know, Frederick Olyphant was the special pictorial correspondent of the *Gotham Gazette* all through the little unpleasantness between the turbaned Turk and the Russian bear. I did not get out there to see him until near the end of the tussle. Then I heard an allusion to the man with the Black Heart, and I asked Fred for full particulars. At first he was a recalcitrant witness, but I managed to get at the main facts by dint of hard labor; and here they are:

"Frederick Olyphant was with the Russian troops all through the terrible winter campaign. As the representative of an important newspaper and as an American, he was doubly welcome, and his labors were made as pleasant for him as possible. The Russian officers were as friendly as he could wish, and he was allowed special privileges. One day he was with the advance guard as it entered a little town called Tartar-Bazardjik. Just as Fred was going to get some-

thing to eat, he saw a squad of soldiers dragging
off a poor devil to instant execution. The man
had been caught looting. Now, there was no
end of stealing in those days; your teeth were
not safe in your head if you slept with your
mouth open; and the Russian officers had orders
to stop it short, and to shoot any man caught in
the act. Fred had seen lots of poor wretches,
half-a-dozen at a time, stood up against a blank
wall and dropped with a single volley from a
company detailed for the purpose. It was not
his business to interfere. But something about
this man in Bazardjik attracted his attention, and
as the soldiers passed him he looked at the
fellow carefully. There was an air of pride
about the man, despite his desperate condition;
his eye, as it glanced about like that of a hunted
beast, was as sharp as a needle; plainly enough
the fellow was not a vulgar thief. Acting on a
sudden impulse, Fred determined to save the
man's life. Throwing up his hand, and speaking
as one having authority, he commanded the
men to halt! The Russian soldier is as docile
as he is brave, and he is used to being ordered
about sharply. The soldiers who were leading
the man away to death stopped short and saluted
Fred, whom they took for an officer of high
rank, judging from his manner. Their captive
drew himself up and looked at Fred. It was the
look of a man who did not fear death, although

he longed for life. Fred asked the corporal, who was in command of the little squad of soldiers, what the fellow had been doing. He had been caught stealing bread, the Russian answered. Now, in those troublesome times to loot food was no great crime; Fred had done it himself, when he had to choose between starvation and a helping of himself without so much as a by-your-leave. So he determined to save the prisoner. 'The man is my servant,' he said to the soldiers, 'let him go. I will chastise him.' And as the Russians released him, Fred, he struck him across the shoulders with his whip, and called him a dog, and ordered him to carry the baggage up stairs. The corporal and his men hesitated a little as they saw their prey pass from their hands, but Fred paid no attention to their murmurings, and ordered his new servant harshly, and struck him again once or twice, to disarm suspicion, until at last the soldiers yielded and made off."

" Really, now," ventured Mr. Hobson-Chol-mondeley," did Mr. Olyphant truly save a man's life ? "

" Well, he did," Uncle Larry replied.

" What has this to do with the Black Heart ? " asked Rudolph Vernon.

" Well, I'll tell you, if you will give me time ;" and Uncle Larry lighted one of the tiny little cigars he always affected.

"Gentlemen of The Full Score!" cried Charley Sutton, "silence for the Chair!"

Uncle Larry took a long pull at his little cigar and then went on:

"While Fred was ordering about the man he had rescued, he was sizing him up and taking stock of him. And he wasn't any too pleased with the result of his observations. The man was apparently a Greek. He had small black eyes, given to quick underhand glances; but, as Fred thought, this furtive look might be due to the desperate strait the man was in. He had a little pointed black mustache, under which there was a gleam of teeth seen through a treacherous smile. He had a dead white face and in the centre of his forehead he had a birth-mark, a curious stain in the shape of a human heart. Fred found out after, that when the man was not excited this red scar burned and blazed on his forehead like the gory socket of the Cyclops' eye. But at all times of mental strain, the birth-mark became surcharged with blood, and it sank deeper and darker into the white skin, until at last there stood out on the man's forehead a black heart!"

"And didn't Fred ever discover who the fellow was, and where he came from?" asked Eliphalet Duncan.

"Well, he did," Laurence Laughton replied. "The man's name was Constantine Vollonides.

He was a Levantine Greek, and his mother had been a Corsican."

"If he was a Corsican by descent and a Levantine by training, he was prepared both by heredity and by environment to cherish revenge as a sacred duty, and not to be scrupulous in its attainment." This was the contribution of Mr. Rudolph Vernon, whose poetry was sometimes super-saturated with scientific phraseology.

"You have rung the bell this time," said Uncle Larry. "Constantine Vollonides was an incarnation of the vendetta, and he was as free from all scruple as only a Levantine can be; and, more than this, he was a Greek, with the intolerable pride of a Greek, and with all the sensitiveness which accompanies that pride. He had a feeling of humiliation that he had been forced to accept a menial position from Fred, even though it was to save his life. And he never forgave Fred for the few light blows given him in the presence of the soldiers to lessen their suspicion. He felt degraded at the thought that there was a man living whom he had called master, and who had struck him."

"But didn't the fellow see that Fred had done this only in the hope of saving his life?" asked Eliphalet Duncan.

"Well, I don't know," said Uncle Larry; "he may have seen it well enough; I suppose he did; but it made no difference. It was no let or hindrance to the hatred he bore Fred ever after."

"Of course," remarked Eliphalet Duncan, "but he had other motives for his hatred, too!"

"He had," answered Uncle Larry, "or at least his existing hatred was greatly intensified by a little episode which took place a few hours after Fred first met him. As Fred's apparent servant, Vollonides got knowledge of the hiding-place of a kindly old Turkish gentleman whom Fred was also trying to shield; and out of pure cussedness, apparently, and with incredible meanness, the Greek betrayed this Turk to the Russians, and the old gentleman was most brutally ill-treated; in fact, he died from his injuries. Of course, when Fred heard of this he was wild, and he just gave Vollonides a piece of his mind. Fred told the fellow he had intervened in his behalf out of no kindness to him, and that he regretted already what he had done, and that he had saved his worthless life only as he would have saved the life of any other wretched cur. Now, Fred can use early English when he tries, and he let the Greek have it hot and heavy. And if Vollonides had hated Fred before, for the blows of the whip, he hated him after with a ten-fold hatred, because of the stinging scorn with which he had been lashed."

"Truly, a most unpleasant person, I should say," remarked Mr. Hobson-Cholmondeley.

" And what might his position be?—I mean was he a man of family ? "

" I believe he had not a little pride of birth, and he was a man of some small means, too; he was full of splendid financial schemes, and it was in spying out the land to prospect for one of these that he had got caught between the lines and robbed and left for dead. In the desperation of hunger he had taken the bread, for the theft of which the Russians were going to shoot him. Oddly enough, he never bore malice against the soldiers who arrested him. On the contrary, he hated the Turk as only a Greek can. As soon as he could get off scart-free he left Fred, without a word of thanks; and the next time we heard of him, he had been the chief instrument of the surprise and capture by the Russians of an important Turkish fort, impregnable except against treachery. You see, he was no coward, and no common villain, though he was as capable of mischief and as capable in making mischief as Iago or the Prince of Darkness himself."

" It is a pity," suggested Eliphalet Duncan, " that Fred, who has some superstitions, had not yet another,—that he did not share the unwillingness of the inhabitants of the northern coasts of Scotland, who hesitate to help a drowning man, for fear that they may be made responsible for the support and care of the man whose life they have saved."

"You have told us about the first meeting between Fred and the man with the Black Heart," said Charley Sutton, "now shed some light on the second."

"Turn yourself full on, Uncle Larry, and give us the latest news and all the particulars," urged Bob White.

"Well," said Uncle Larry, "at the tail-end of the war, when peace was certain and we were all making ready to go our several ways, we got up a dinner over in Perà,—a few Americans, a lot of correspondents and some of our particular friends among the Russian officers. Vollonides was in Constantinople then, and one of the officers brought him to the dinner. He made himself pleasant enough until he caught sight of Fred, and then the blood rushed to his forehead, and I saw the black heart for the first time. Generally, Vollonides was a man of easy conversation, but that evening he was ugly and as cantankerous a cuss as the devil could find anywhere to do his dirty work. The Russian officers had began to know his ways and to find out his peculiarities; and one of them leaned over to me and whispered 'When you see the black heart,—beware!' From this officer I pumped a lot of facts about Constantine Vollonides, how he had been making money, hand over fist, how he had half-a-dozen financial schemes on foot, how he was establishing in business the chief members of his family, how he had one brother in Southern California."

"You don't say so?" interrupted Charley Sutton; "down in Old California?"

"Down on the peninsula somewhere," answered Laughton. "I got my information from a Russian; and, of course, he didn't know California from Kalamazoo."

"Proceed,—your story interests me strangely," said J. Warren Payn, in apt parody of the mannerisms of the latest imported tragedian.

Uncle Larry started his little cigar again, and continued:

"When I was warned against this Constantine Vollonides, I took notice of him, and I saw that he kept glancing stealthily at Fred, and it struck me that his expression was very vindictive. This surprised me, and I doubted what I saw, because it seemed to me impossible that a man should bear malice against another man for saving his life. I ought to tell you that the room we were in had been decorated by two or three of the residents with flags and arms, and with any number of pictures of scenes in the war, cut from the illustrated papers. Among these was a full page portrait of Constantine Vollonides, published in the *Illustrated London News* just after he had made himself known by his services to the Russian cause. And, of course, there were lots and lots of Fred's sketches. One of the correspondents said something to Vollonides about one of these sketches of Fred's, and Vollonides made some disparaging remark. The correspondent protested, and Vollonides repeated his remark, out loud, so that everybody could hear it. Fred couldn't help hearing it; but he didn't let on or take notice. Then Vollonides began to criticise Fred's sketches, one by one, in a most offensive manner. Fortunately, they were at opposite ends of the table, and down at our end we made as much noise as we could to try and drown his remarks. But it was no use. He stood up before one picture and declared that it could only have been drawn by a coward, skulking out of the line of danger. Then the officer who had invited him tried to get him to keep quiet; but that wasn't any use either. The man was set on having his own will."

"Do you mean to say," asked Mr. Hobson-Cholmondeley, as Laughton paused to take a fresh cigar, "that the fellow really wanted to pick a quarrel with the man who had saved his life?"

"He couldn't wait to pick a quarrel," returned Uncle Larry; "he just took up any quarrel that was handy; and if one didn't come handy, he meant to make it. At last he insulted Fred so grossly that notice had to be taken of it; I needn't tell you what the insult was, for it was as low in its expression as it was malignant in its intent. Fred felt that as an American among

strangers it was his duty to speak up. He asked
me to go across the room and demand an apology.
Constantine Vollonides smiled a sinister smile of
self-satisfaction as I came up to him, and referred
me to the officer whose guest he was. This
officer was a gentleman, and a very disgusted man
he was indeed ; but he was powerless. Vollonides
refused to apologize, and it was arranged that the
meeting should take place on the spot."

" A duel ? " asked Rudolph Vermon, eagerly.

" That was the size of it," responded Larry.

" A duel—in a room—across a handkerchief, in
the regular old fashion ? I should have joyed to
see it," cried the poet.

" Well, I don't know," said Uncle Larry, "a
duel is all very well to read about or to hear
about, but it isn't any fun when it's your best
friend who is going to stand up to be shot at."

" Why did they fight in the room ? " asked
Charley Sutton.

" For several reasons. The insult had been
public, and it was only fair that those who had
heard it should be present at the meeting. Then,
many of those at the dinner were going off and
away the next morning. Then, too, secrecy and
despatch were necessary, and there was no place
where we could get these better than the room
we were in—a long, large room, big enough to
serve as the banqueting hall for a state dinner."

"And they fought a duel in a dining-room ? "

inquired Mr. Hobson-Cholmondeley, with deep anxiety.

"They fought a duel across the dining-room table!" said Uncle Larry.

"Dear me!" sighed Mr. Hobson-Cholmondeley; "how very dreadful!"

"Of course, Fred did not want to fight the fellow," continued Uncle Larry, "and he had me declare that he would be satisfied without an apology, if Vollonides would withdraw the opprobrious epithets. The Greek refused with a scornful laugh. I never saw any human being look as devilish as he did, when he laughed then, with that black heart burned deep into his forehead like a brand of Cain. He wanted swords; but we chose revolvers, with only one chamber loaded. The men were to stand on opposite sides of the dinner-table, about ten paces apart, At the word they were to have the right to fire. either where they stood, or after advancing to the table midway between them."

"That's almost as deadly a duel as a fight with bowie-knives in a dark cabin," Charley Sutton remarked.

"As Fred took his place, with his revolver in his right hand, he asked Vollonides to withdraw the insult. 'Are you afraid to face me?' was the only answer he got from the Greek. Fred repeated his request in a manly and dignified way, making a last appeal to avoid bloodshed, if pos-

sible. You see, most the men there had seen
Fred under fire, and they knew he was no coward,
so he could go farther for the sake of peace than
his pride would perhaps have let him go at
another time. And again Vollonides scoffed at
him. ' Are we babies,' he asked, ' that we should
waste time in idle talk? No. I will not retract
what I said. I will repeat it!' And he did.
Well, Fred, he stood still and silent a moment,
and then he said, ' I have given you a last chance
to save your life. Now I shall shoot you through
the heart!' It wasn't at all like Fred to boast,
but the man had outraged him and he meant
what he said."

"And did he do it?" J. Warren Payn asked,
with excited interest.

"Who is telling this tale; you or I?" inquired
Laurence Laughton, sarcastically. "If I am
telling it, let me tell it in my own way."

"Take your time, Uncle Larry," said Poor
Bob White; "so long as we are in at the death
at last, we are in no hurry."

"Well," Laughton continued, "Fred stood on
one side of the room and Vollonides at the other,
and the dining-table divided the distance between
them. The rest of us gathered at the two ends
of the room. I let the officer, who was the
second of Vollonides, give the signal. He asked
them if they were ready. Then he counted, One,
Two, Three—Fire! At the word a swift sound

slit the air; Vollonides had fired at Fred and missed him. The bullet had grazed Fred's ear, and then had lodged itself deep in the wall behind his head. Fred had reserved his fire. He was quite calm and collected. He walked slowly up to the table, and then covered Vollonides with the point of his pistol. I will say for the fellow that he was not a coward. He stood up firmly and he looked Fred in the eye. His face was whiter than ever, and the black heart in his forehead was blacker than ever, but he did not tremble. Fred kept the revolver aimed at the man's breast for at least ten seconds; it seemed an hour to us. What it must have been to the Greek I can only guess."

"Why didn't Fred shoot him dead?" asked Charley Sutton.

"But that would have been murder!" ejaculated the horrified Mr. Hobson-Cholmondeley.

"He said he was going to plug him in the heart," pursued the young Californian. "Why didn't he do it?"

"Well, I don't know," said Uncle Larry; "perhaps he thought it would be too cold-blooded a deed. Perhaps he did not want to take away the life he had saved once already. Yet he had said he would shoot him through the heart. That was why he hesitated so long. Then he slowly raised his revolver until it covered the birthmark on the Greek's forehead. Vollonides did

7

not quail; he looked right along the barrel into
Fred's eye. Then Fred raised the revolver a
little higher yet and fired and sent his bullet into
the left breast of the portrait of Constantine
Vollonides—the portrait which hung right over
the head of the original!"

"Fancy now!" said Mr. Hobson-Cholmondeley.

"So the accused escaped on a technicality,"
suggested Eliphalet Duncan, the lawyer.

"Fred would have done better if he had
dropped him in his tracks," Charley Sutton
remarked.

"I understand well enough why he let him
go," Rudolph Vernon declared; "but the story
would have been more picturesque, more poetic,
if he had killed him."

"It was a very close call for Fred," resumed
Charley Sutton.

"Well, it was," said Uncle Larry; "if the
Greek's bullet had gone an inch to the right, it
would have found its billet in Fred's head. Fred
has the bullet now; I dug it out of the wall and
gave it to him. He had it mounted in a gold
vulture's claw, and he wears it on his watch-
chain.

"Didn't the fellow want to fight again?"
asked Charley Sutton, for whom all tales of
mortal combat had a morbid fascination.

"Well, he wanted to fight," Uncle Larry went

on; " he was full of fight, but his friends refused to let him, and at last they had to take him away. He passed near Fred as he went out, and he said, ' We have met twice, and twice my life has been in your hands; the third time, your life will be in mine, and I shall not spare it, unless I can find a punishment worse than death!'"

" He was a cheerful person for a small dinner-party," said Bob White, " Let us rejoice that he does not belong to The Full Score."

" He was a regular old-time villain," Charley Sutton added. "' Ha, ha! a time will come!'"

" And was that the last you saw of him?" Rudolph Vernon asked.

" I never saw him again, and I am quite sure Fred. has not, either," answered Larry.

" And where is he now?" urged Charley Sutton.

" In heaven, perhaps," Uncle Larry replied, " or in the other place. I don't know, and as long as I am in this world, I don't care."

" I think that if I were Fred," Rudolph Vernon declared, " I should not feel safe while that man was alive."

" Neither should I," assented Mr. Hobson-Cholmondeley.

" I should always be afraid," continued the poet, " that sooner or later that Greek would turn up and stab me in the back."

"Fred is not afraid," replied Uncle Larry, "because he does not know what it is to fear any man. He is superstitious, you know, and if he fears anything, it is the unknown. Besides, he is something of a fatalist, and he is inclined to cry Kismet—it is Fate!"

"All the same," said Charley Sutton, "he must think sometimes about the man with the Black Heart. A fellow never could forget an experience like his!"

"And Fred does think of it," rejoined Rudolph Vernon; "don't you remember what he said to-day at dinner before Uncle Larry told us the story? He said that if he were to be killed to-night, or if he were to disappear mysteriously, his death or his disappearance would lie at the door of a man whose life he had saved."

"Surely, you do not think the Greek would dare to follow him to this country?" inquired Mr. Hobson-Cholmondeley.

"The man's a Levantine," replied Rudolph Vernon, "half Greek and half Corsican. There is no limit to the journey he might take to accomplish his revenge."

"*C'est curieux! c'est très curieux,*" ventured Mr. Hobson-Cholmondeley.

"I say, Uncle Larry," Charley Sutton asked, "when was this duel?"

"In 1878."

"And we are in October, 1884—six years.

Perhaps by this time the man with the Black Heart is dead."

" Perhaps he is," answered Uncle Larry, as his guests rose from the table and passed into the library; all but two or three, who had begun a discussion on æsthetics, which bade fair to be interminable.

CHAPTER VII.

AFTER DINNER.

IN the library they found Frederick Olyphant seated at the desk-table in the centre of the room. He had written his letter, and he was engaged in sealing the envelope with wax, which he stamped with the leaden bullet grasped in a golden vulture's claw. Ever since he had worn the miscarrying messenger of death as a charm on his watch-chain, he had taken pleasure in using it as a seal. It gave a firm impression of a hollow sphere; and it was at once simple and unique, two qualities which the artist held in the highest esteem.

As Laurence Laughton stood by the broad, flat desk, Olyphant looked up and held up his letter. "Would the faithful Bridget post this for me, Uncle Larry? I couldn't rest till I had written it, and I'd like to see it off as soon as possible."

"Of course she would," responded the host, touching the button of an electric bell, which was immediately heard to tinkle sharply somewhere in the dim recesses of the basement. "The faithful Bridget has taken a great fancy to you, Fred, and she will run to the corner lamp-post with it, if the cook and the waiters have gone,— and I suppose they have by this time, for the faithful Bridget bundles them out as soon as she can."

The faithful Bridget was the chief of Uncle Larry's household. She was an Irishwoman, now long past middle age, who had come to Laurence's mother thirty years before, as cook. She ruled the house with a mild despotism under which Laughton was sometimes restive. Although she had two assistants to aid her in her household labors, she still prepared the few simple meals which the master of the house took at home. She resented not a little the intrusion of the professional cooks and waiters who served the more elaborate repasts which Laurence Laughton offered his friends, and she sent them away the instant that their work was done. The faithful Bridget was herself indefatigable and she took pride in her housekeeping. She was known to most of the frequenters of the house, for she generally opened the door herself.

As she came into the library in answer to Laughton's ring, she was greeted with a chorus : " Hello, Bridget," " How are you, my aged darling?" " She looks younger every day, so she does!" Mr. Hobson-Cholmondeley listened in perturbed surprise; but the faithful Bridget received these pleasantries with amiable scorn. "Good evening to yez, gintlemin," was all she said.

"Bridget, Mr. Olyphant wants to know if it would be too much trouble to ask you to post a letter for him before you go to bed?" asked the master of the house, with the courtesy he always showed to servants.

"Sure it's no trouble at all," answered Bridget; "and it's many a mile I'd walk for Mr. Frederick, let alone going to the corner here!"

"I shall be very much obliged to you, indeed," said Olyphant, handing her the letter.

"I'll take it over at once," she said, "and then it's going to bed I am. These dinners and these waiters and these cooks are a-wearing the life out of me."

As she withdrew to the regions below, White said, "Larry, you are under petticoat government! The faithful Bridget rules you with a rod of iron. You dare not say your soul is your own!"

"What man *may* say that?" asked Fred, coming to his friend's assistance.

"What man is bulldozed by a faithful Bridget?" rejoined White. "Why, Uncle Larry, thou art the man. Now, I would not allow any Bridget to rule my roast. I abjure the Hibernian. When I advertise for a cook, I shall add, that, like the Government of these United States, I reserve the right to reject all Bids."

Before the sudden shower of groans which greeted this merry jest, Poor Bob White retreated into the parlor, taking with him Mr. J. Warren Payn. They opened the piano and betook themselves to music; Mr. Hobson-Cholmondeley joined them; he had written the words of a sweetly sentimental French song, and Mr. J. Warren Payn had set them to music for him.

" I'm not quite satisfied with the accompaniment yet," said the composer, " but I will try it for you."

" You may venture the *experimentum in corpore vilo*," responded Mr. Hobson-Cholmondeley, with scholarly jocularity.

" That's Latin, I take it," remarked Mr. Robert White, " for ' try it on a dog'; isn't it ? "

" Really," replied the little Englishman, with a faint smile, rubbing his hands together nervously, " you have so many of these Americanisms that I can't pretend to keep up with them all."

" I'm not quite sure," the composer continued, as he played the introduction, " that the air I have written is absolutely original."

" Probably it isn't," White interrupted: " now-a-days nothing *is* original except sin. And in music, I believe plagiarism is not a sin."

" Let us hope it is not an unpardonable sin," said Mr. Hobson-Cholmondeley, uneasily.

One or two other members of The Full Score, hearing the first notes of the new song, lounged

from the library into the parlor and joined the
little group about the piano. The door which
opened into the parlor from the hall folded back
against the piano, and as this inconvenienced
White, he closed it, and made more room about
the instrument.

There was another little knot of men in the
dining-room, where the discussion of æstheticism
had drifted slowly into a debate on international
manners.

"My definition of politeness is very simple,"
Rudolph Vernon was declaring, with emphasis;
"and yet it is comprehensive. Politeness is the
outward and visible sign of an inward and
spiritual grace."

"Of course, but what do you suggest as a
means of grace?" asked Eliphalet Duncan, who,
as a half-Scotchman, took a keen interest in
considering the minor points of theological
metaphysics.

"But that definition won't help you any,"
ventured Charley Sutton, "when you are having high words and passing low language with
the driver of a growler in London at two o'clock
in the morning, and there's no policeman in
sight."

"There is no international standard of manners,
and it is unfortunate," continued the poet. "Every
people has its own conventionalities. Now the
beauty of my definition is that it takes a lofty

view, that it soars above these lesser and often very little points of difference, and that it goes right to the essentials."

"It is hard to frame a definition of an English gentleman," Eliphalet Duncan remarked, "which does not fit an American tramp quite as well. It must turn on abstinence from work."

Rudolph Vernon quoted :

"When Adam delve and Eve span
Who was then the gentleman ? "

"I like Davy Crockett's definition best," added Charley Sutton. "He said General Jackson was a perfect gentleman ; he set the whiskey-jug on the table and looked the other way!"

"In England they think not only that a man is no gentleman, but that he is going to the devil if he does not wear a high hat on Sunday," said Eliphalet Duncan.

"And in France a man wears a dress-coat in the morning to a wedding, and he puts on white kids when he goes to ' propose.' " This contribution to sociological science came from Charley Sutton.

"Who was it said," Rudolph Vernon asked, "that it was only the very highest civilization which permits the high hat, the glass eye and the false tooth?"

"I don't see why all nations cannot dwell together in unity," Charley Sutton suggested;

"let's be a happy family, as the monkey said to the parrot."

"In my experience, now," Rudolph Vernon began, "I give it to you for what it is worth—"

"If you are going to give us your experience, I don't object," interrupted Charley Sutton, "but do not offer to lend it to us. I have found that experience is like a dress-coat; it never fits anybody but the owner."

In the course of a few minutes the little knot of disputants in the dining-room, and the little group about the piano in the parlor, gradually absorbed all the members of The Full Score, except Frederick Olyphant and Laurence Laughton, who were left alone in the library, sitting before the hearth, whereon a cheery blaze of hickory sparkled and sang.

"You are out of sorts this evening, aren't you?" asked Laughton, with the fatherly interest he always felt toward Olyphant.

"I am, indeed," Fred answered, quickly; "how could I help feeling miserable when I—" He checked himself suddenly, flushed a little and said, "But I have made amends now, and I shall sleep better for it."

Laughton had no desire to pry into his friend's secrets; but he could not help suspecting that the sending of the letter had given relief to his friend's unwonted excitement.

"That is," continued Olyphant, "if I sleep at

all, which I doubt. My mind is easier now, but my body rebels. I have a dull pain in my head, and I feel a feverish irritation."

"You have been driving your machinery too hard," said Uncle Larry. "How is the picture getting on?"

"Do you mean 'The Sharpness of Death'?" the artist asked; "it's nearly done; in fact, it is quite done, if I could only convince myself of it."

"Then take my advice. Drop it for ten days; spend a week in the Adirondacks. To-morrow is the first of November, and it's perhaps a little late for camping out, but it won't hurt two old campaigners like us."

"Would you go with me?"

"Why not?"

Olyphant knew that Laughton had important and pressing engagements early in November, and he was touched with the willingness to lay aside business at the call of friendship.

"It is very kind of you, Uncle Larry," he said, "and I should be delighted to go with you but—but I cannot leave New York for a minute now."

"Your work will be all the better for your vacation."

"Oh, it is not my work—it is—well, I cannot tell you why I must not go. I hope to be able to tell you soon. But there is no use in talking to me about a trip out of town; I am in New York

now, and I shall stay in New York till the spring
and then—well, then, something will happen, I
hope!"

"Beware how you bend the bow till it break!"
Uncle Larry suggested, with kindly interest in
his tone. "All work and no play isn't a good
scheme of living for any man."

"Oh, I have play enough," returned Fred,
"and I do not suppose I work so very hard,
either. I wonder sometimes whether I have
accomplished anything at all, or whether I ever
shall accomplish anything. We little men of
to-day toil on, each in our little groove; we dig
each in our special little trench, throwing up the
earth at the sides, until we half believe we are
twice as deep as we are. I stand up in my little
ditch sometimes and look out over my little mounds
at the broad world around me, and I wonder
whether the result of my work has not been to
hide me from the rest of the people. And worse
yet, I wonder whether the work itself was worth
doing, and whether I have done it as well as I
could, and whether I have put into it the best I
had to give; and then, when I look at the things I
have painted, and when I acknowledge that I have
done my best, I feel what a shallow trifler I am,
straying along the margin of the limitless universe."

"I suppose every man has moments of
profound discouragement and self-questioning,"
said Laughton, gravely.

"Do you think so?" asked Fred. "Do you believe other men are conscious that they had done their best, and then wonder whether their best were worth doing at all?"

"I am sure of it," Uncle Larry answered.

"Then I have partners in my misery," Fred rejoined. "That is some comfort."

"Just look at that fire," said Uncle Larry, starting forward to reconstruct it. "Only a minute or two ago, it was blazing as merrily as may be, and now it is as despondent as you are. A hickory fire on a modern hearth needs as many delicate attentions as the latest fine lady, and it puts on as many airs, and is as variable and as moody. Rudolph Vernon could write a poem on the total depravity of the hickory,— although as the hickory is fore-ordained to the flames, I don't know what else was to have been expected from it." Uncle Larry knelt by the hearth as he turned a glowing stick between the andirons and lifted two others across it. Then two or three judicious whiffs of the bellows blew them into a blaze. As Laughton saw the success of his skillful efforts, he felt the pride which is the chief characteristic of all fire-makers from the time of Prometheus to the present. "There," he said, "there, Fred; look at that! There's a blaze for you! There's a fiery furnace to roast the blue devils out of you. What do you say to that?"

He rose to his feet and restored the bellows to its pendent place beside the tongs. Not hearing from Fred any response to his queries, he turned to see the cause of his silence. The chair in which Olyphant had been sitting was empty. Suddenly it struck Laughton that as he had dropped a heavy stick of hickory on the andirons, he had heard Fred say, " I'll be back in a minute." He recalled this dimly and doubtfully; and, at best, it was a vague impression. He wondered why Fred should leave him in the middle of an interesting chat, breaking off abruptly their discussion of the reason of things. It was not like Fred to do that. He made sure that the painter had joined the men in the dining-room. Perhaps Fred had felt a recurrence of his oppression, and had gone into the dining-room for a glass of water or a drop of a more stimulating beverage. There was no reason why Laughton should follow Olyphant about from room to room, although he confessed to himself a secret uneasiness, due in part to Fred's morbid despondency, and still more to his physical oppression. Laughton feared that the artist had overworked himself, and that he had over-worried about his work. Fred was a sturdy fellow, and he was in excellent condition, but there is a strain which will crush the strongest and the soundest.

Uncle Larry had been standing with his back

to the fire as he made these reflections. Almost involuntarily he walked to the wide doorway which connected the library and the dining-room. There the little group of talkers still clustered about one end of the dining-room; and from æstheticism and politeness the discussion had drifted to temperance.

"I don't take any stock in the Blue Ribbon crowd," Charley Sutton was saying. "They think drink is at the bottom of all the deviltry in the world. Now, that, if you will excuse the poor pun, is an argument *post hock ergo propter hock.*"

"Let him die a lingering death," cried the horror-stricken Rudolph Vernon. "Hale him away to the deepest dungeon neath the castle moat. Two deaths were not punishment enough for one pun."

"Have you such a thing as a dungeon in the house, Uncle Larry?" Eliphalet Duncan queried, as he looked up and saw his host standing beside him.

"Where is Fred?" Laughton asked, too pre-occupied to hear or to heed the question put to him.

"He hasn't been in here since dinner," answered Duncan. "I thought he was in the library talking to you."

"So he was until a few minutes ago. Then he slipped out, and I supposed he might have come in here, or at least passed through."

8

" Of course," replied Duncan, " he might have
been seen in here, but we haven't seen him at all ;
and he could not have passed through the room
because I closed the door into the hall just after
dinner on account of the draught, and it has not
been opened since."

Laughton saw that the little group was
gathered at the end of the dinner table, very near
the door into the hall, and they were so seated
that even had the door been open no one could
have passed them to go out without disturbing
the whole party. He knew, too, that the door,
which was a sliding one, was a little out of repair,
and moved slowly and with a harsh noise. He
felt sure, therefore, that Fred had not gone out
through the dining-room. He remained a few
minutes in humorous chat. Then he began to
wonder why Fred did not return, if he really
had said, " I'll be back in a minute." As soon
as he could break loose from the jolly circle in
the dining-room Laughton walked through the
library into the parlor, expecting to see Fred
among those gathered about the piano.

But Olyphant was nowhere to be seen.

As Laughton entered the room, Mr. Hobson-
Cholmondeley was singing the last stanza of a
ballad of Heine's. When the music ceased,
Uncle Larry asked Robert White, who was lean-
ing against the door into the hall, " Where is
Fred ? "

"I don't know," answered Poor Bob White, facetiously; "I haven't got him concealed about my person. You may search me, if you like, and I will submit to the indignity."

"How long is it since he went out?" was Laughton's next question.

"Has he gone out?" returned White, seriously, seeing, by Laughton's look, that jocularity was misplaced at that moment.

"Why, didn't he pass through here to go out into the hall a few minutes ago?" asked Uncle Larry, with great surprise.

"No," answered White. "Nobody has gone through this door, since we began to have a little music, for I have been leaning against it all the time. And beside, Fred hasn't even been in here since dinner."

Then where had he gone? And how had he left the library?

Laurence Laughton opened the door against which White had been leaning, and called loudly, "Fred! Fred!" Then after a pause he called again, "Fred!"

But there was no answer to his cry.

CHAPTER VIII.

A STRANGE COINCIDENCE.

MR. HOBSON-CHOLMONDELEY noted the expression of puzzled surprise on Laurence Laughton's face, as he closed the door into the hall. "*Qu'est-ce qu'il y a?*" he asked, at once. "Has anything happened?"

"Well, I don't know," answered Uncle Larry; "perhaps, and again, perhaps not. But the fact is that Olyphant has disappeared."

"Why shouldn't he?" White demanded. "This is a free country, and the constitution guarantees to every man the right to disappear whenever he likes."

"Is there anything strange in Olyphant's going away, that you seem so put out, Uncle Larry," asked Mr. J. Warren Payn, turning about on the piano-stool.

"There is nothing so strange in his leaving us," replied Larry, doubtfully; "I half expected him to go early, as he was not feeling well."

"Well, then," began White.

"But what is strange," continued Laughton,

" is the method of his going. In fact, I don't see how he got out at all ! "

" I suppose he walked out," White suggested, "just as we all walked in, through the door."

" But the doors were closed," said Larry, with a little impatience.

" *This* door was closed," White admitted; " I can bear witness to the fact that he did not go out through this room, but there's a door from the dining-room into the hall, isn't there ? "

" That door was shut too," returned Larry, "and Sutton and Duncan were sitting so close to it that nobody could get by."

" I am ready to take my Alfred-David that he did not make his exit by this door," repeated White.

" So am I," declared Mr. J. Warren Payn.

" *Moi aussi,*" Mr. Hobson-Cholmondeley added.

" Let's take a look at the other door," White suggested, and the rest of the party followed him through the library into the dining-room.

As they entered, Charley Sutton looked up and asked.

" What was Fred doing in the other room, Uncle Larry ? "

" Well, I don't know," answered Uncle Larry ; " because he wasn't there at all."

" If he wasn't there, where was he ? " returned the young Californian.

" That's just what we are trying to find out,"
rejoined White. " Have you and Duncan been
sitting just as you are for long ? "

" We have been here nearly an hour, I take it,"
Duncan answered.

" Without moving ? "

" Without a move," said Sutton.

" And Fred didn't go out through that door ? "

" Of course, he did not," replied Duncan.

" Who said he did ? " Charley Sutton added.

" You see, it is exactly as I told you," said
Uncle Larry.

Mr. Hobson-Cholmondeley gazed about the
dining-room in wonder, and remarked, " It is
most extraordinary, most extraordinary, indeed."

" You do not mean to suggest that Fred has
vanished ? " asked Rudolph Vernon—" gone and
left no sign ? "

" That is exactly what he has done," Uncle
Larry explained. "He was talking with me here
in the library.   Then I leant forward to rearrange
the fire.   When I sat down again, Fred was gone.
I have an indistinct impression that while I was
attending to the hickory I heard him say, ' I'll be
back in a minute ! ' but I cannot be sure about
this ; I was not paying attention to him just then,
and I recall his words, if they were his words,
only in the vaguest way.   When he did not return,
I came for him here in the dining-room ; but he
was not here, and you said he had not been here."

" Not since dinner," Vernon declared.

" Then I went into the parlor," continued Uncle Larry, " and he had not been there, either. And if he has not left these rooms through the parlor-door or the dining-room door, how has he left them ? That's what I want to know."

" He hasn't taken French leave, you know— thawed and resolved himself into adieu, has he ? " Mr. Hobson-Cholmondeley ventured to inquire ; but most of those present took a serious interest in Olyphant's disappearance, and therefore ignored the little Englishman's little joke.

Robert White had been standing on the rug before the fire in the library, the spot on which Fred Olyphant had last been seen. He was considering carefully the means of exit from the three rooms : " If he had opened the windows in either the parlor or the dining-room, we should have seen him, and heard him, and felt the draught. And I know he did not cross the parlor to go to the window."

" And I am as sure that he did not cross the dining-room to go to the window," declared Rudolph Vernon.

Mr. Hobson-Cholmondeley took his stand on the rug by the side of White ; he was rubbing his hands together gently, and he wore a puzzled smile as he strenuously applied his logical faculty to the solution of the problem. " I suppose there isn't a door going into the

hall from this library, now?" he queried, insinu-
atingly.

"But there is!" answered White; "of course,
there is; and it is concealed behind that curtain
there, across the opening in the bookcase
opposite us."

"Well, I don't know," said Uncle Larry,
"that you need bother about that little door,
because it is locked, and the key is up stairs in
my room."

"Let's see, if it is locked now," suggested
White, who was a true journalist, and who
therefore had a full share of the detective
faculty.

He crossed the library, and lifting the light
curtain which masked the passage through the
bookcase, he tried to open the door into the hall.
It was locked.

Perhaps a diagram of the first floor of Laurence Laughton's house showing the arrangement
of the parlor, library and dining-room, will make
the peculiar conditions of the puzzle which the
members of The Full Score were trying to solve
a little clearer to the reader.

"This door is locked now," said White; "but
was it locked a little while ago?"

"Is it locked now?" echoed Mr. Hobson-
Cholmondeley.

"It is always kept locked," Uncle Larry
answered.

" Hasn't it been open at all?" persisted the journalist.

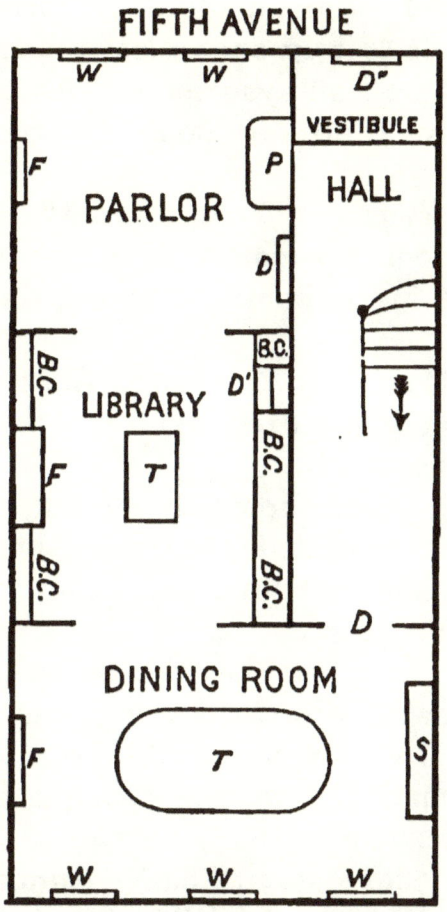

W—Windows. F—Fire-places. P—Piano. S—Sideboard. T—Tables.
D—Doors.   D'—Little door in bookcase of Library hidden behind
curtain. B-C—Bookcases. D''—Street door.

"Of course," said Eliphalet Duncan, " it must have been open some time or other."

" It was unlocked early in the week," the host declared, " when the faithful Bridget had this floor cleaned. I found the door open, and told Bridget to lock it up and to leave the key in my bureau, where I always keep it. As the door is locked now, I do not doubt that the key is in my room."

" *Voulez-vous que je vous dise ?* " Mr. Hobson-Cholmondeley remarked in his deep voice ; " I believe Mr. Olyphant went out through this little door."

" But it is locked," retorted Charley Sutton ; " you don't think Fred went out through the key-hole, do you ? "

" I don't know how he went out, or why he went out," persisted the Englishman, " but directly I saw that little door, I made sure that he went out that way."

" But I have the key which locked it—I'll bring it down," said Uncle Larry, and he opened the door from the parlor into the hall. A sudden exclamation from him brought the others rapidly after him.

" What is it ? " asked Charley Sutton.

" Have you a clue ? " White queried.

" Well, I don't know," said Uncle Larry, " but Fred's hat is gone."

" There's his coat," remarked Rudolph Vernon.

" I see his coat," replied Uncle Larry, " but

his hat has gone. It is an odd-looking head-piece that no one but Fred would dare to wear, and it is not here. He always hung it on one special hook—and this is the hook and there is nothing on it."

"If he took his hat?" asked Vernon, thoughtfully, "why shouldn't he take his coat too?"

Robert White said nothing. He went straight to the door in the hall leading into the library, and tried it from the outside. Beyond all doubt it was locked, and the key had been taken out.

"That isn't half as puzzling as to guess how he got out of the library," responded Charley Sutton. "We know he didn't go through the dining-room; Rudolph here says he didn't pass through the parlor; and the only door in the library is locked. Now, how the devil did he get out? It beats the King's puzzle with the apple-dumplings."

Mr. Hobson-Cholmondeley, with the pugnacious self-assertion of a little man, said: "He came through that door in the book-case. I'll lay you odds he did!"

"Then," returned Uncle Larry, coming down stairs again with the key in his hand, "then he must have gone up through the chimney to get the key, for I found it where I said it was, in the top drawer of my bureau."

"Perhaps he had a key of his own, you know," suggested Mr. Hobson-Cholmondeley

mildly, slightly staggered by the evidence of the
key, and yet clinging to his theory with the
utmost pertinacity.

Charley Sutton laughed. " Do you take Fred
Olyphant for a burglar," he asked, " coming here
to Uncle Larry's with a bunch of false keys in
his pocket? "

" He came out through that little door," Mr.
Hobson-Cholmondeley declared again, as calmly
and firmly as a British square would receive a
charge of French cavalry. " *C'est mon dernier
mot.*"

" There's no use trying to convert Chum,"
acknowledged Charley Sutton ; " when he's sot,
he's sot, and there's an end."

" With some men," Mr. Rudolph Vernon
remarked, judicially, " argument is like a hammer : it only drives in their false opinions more
firmly."

" Let me see the key, Uncle Larry," asked
White, and Laughton handed it to him. He
examined it carefully ; but it told no secrets, if it
had any to tell. He put it in the lock, and it
turned easily and the door opened. From the
hall one could not see into the library because
of the curtain which hung across the opening
in the bookcase. Mr. Hobson-Cholmondeley
went back into the library through the parlor,
and lifting up the curtain of this little door, he
passed out into the hall. " *Voilà,*" he said,

" he left the library by this door. *Ce n'est pas plus difficile que ça !* "

"But the door was locked!" Charley Sutton cried. " Do you think Fred was an Esoteric Buddhist, and that he dematerialized himself and went plumb through the black-walnut panels of the door? "

" The door may not have been locked," Mr. Hobson-Cholmondeley reiterated, " or he may have had a key,—I'm sure I don't know. But I feel it in my bones, you know, that he passed through that door, just like I did a minute ago."

Here White surprised the company by appearing in the doorway on his hands and knees, bearing a candle and examining the carpet.

" Trying to pick up the trail? " asked Charley Sutton, sarcastically.

" Exactly so," answered White, rising to his feet; " I thought I might find a clue—but there is nothing." He set down the candle and stood for a moment in thought. Then he looked carefully up and down the hall and along the staircase. Suddenly his face brightened, and he took three quick strides, which brought him to the door of the vestibule.

" Got it? " asked Charley Sutton.

" Perhaps," was the answer. " Just look here!"

The members of The Full Score crowded

around the journalist as he stood at the end of the hall.

" This inside door is not shut tight," he said.

" That's so," Charley Sutton cried; " it's ajar, a good half inch, too ! "

" What does that prove ? " Vernon inquired.

" It proves nothing," answered White, " but it fits into a theory of mine."

" Out with your theory ! "

" It is slight and incomplete, but you shall have it for what it is worth. Fred was not feeling well, so Uncle Larry told us—"

" He complained of an oppression in the head," explained Laughton, who had been listening silently and sadly to the queries and conjectures of his guests. An expression in his face seemed to indicate that he took the matter to heart more than the others, and that he thought it more serious.

" He had an oppression in the head," White continued, " and he felt the need of fresh air, which might make him feel better. While Uncle Larry was making the fire, he slipped out into the hall—"

" But how ? " asked Vernon.

" How did he get out ? " cried Charley Sutton.

" Through the little door in the library," Mr. Hobson-Cholmondeley repeated, deliberately.

" There I am puzzled," White went on ; " I do not know how he got out of the library. I cannot even guess. But that he did get out some-how is certain, for he was in the library and he is there no longer. Once out here in the hall, he took his hat."

"Are you sure it was there at all?" asked Duncan.

"Yes," responded White, "for I remember seeing it on its customary hook as I came in. He felt an oppression, he needed air, he took his hat and he stepped to the front door. As he did not intend to go home, but only to stand on the steps for a minute or two, he did not put on his overcoat, and he left the inner door ajar that he might come back without ringing."

" Then he may be on the steps now," Vernon suggested.

" Of course he may be, but I doubt it," White responded, opening the inner door and passing into the vestibule He tried to pry open the street-door, without touching the knob, to see if that also had been left ajar. But it was firmly closed. Having made sure of this, the journalist opened the door and stepped out upon the stoop. There was no one there. The chilly azure radiance of the electric light illumined the deserted avenue. Scarcely any one was in sight except a policeman, leisurely walking down on the opposite side, swing-ing his club jauntily, and closing the area-gates.

" He isn't here," said Charley Sutton, following White out on the stoop.

" No!" answered the journalist, gravely, "and I hardly expected to find him here."

" Why not?" asked the Californian. " Don't you take stock in your own theory?"

" My theory only accounted for his going to the door; it did not pretend to explain the reason that he did not return."

" Perhaps he changed his mind and went home."

" Perhaps." This was said doubtfully.

" You don't think so?"

" No," replied White, " I do not. Fred would not have gone without his overcoat; he was too old a campaigner to run risks; he had had too many real hardships to invent new ones, and it would be a hardship to go without an overcoat on a night as cold as this, and after so sudden a fall of temperature. And, more than that, Fred would not have left us without a word. That is not like him."

" Then what do you think?" asked Rudolph Vernon, who had joined them on the stoop.

" I do not like to think at all."

" Are you afraid some harm has come to Fred?" inquired Charley Sutton.

" Why else should he not have come back?" returned White.

" After all," retorted Charley, " we are not sure that he came out; that's only your theory."

" That's all," admitted White.

"And even if he did come out here," continued the Californian, "he may have gone home."

"True," admitted White again; "he may have done so. But,—" and he paused in doubt.

"Well?"

"But I do not think so."

"Then what can have happened?"

"I don't know."

Nothing was said for a few moments. Then Rudolph Vernon, who had stepped to the outer edge of the stoop, waved his hand to the heavens and said, "See the majestic sadness of the solemn night; is it not superb? I never stand out in the nocturnal silence that I do not declare my preference for the Argus eyes of night above the Cyclops eye of day." The poet paused, evidently pleased with his conceit. "Look there!" he said, sharply; and as he pointed they all turned to look up the avenue. High above the horizon, higher than when Fred looked up at it that afternoon as he went to see Winifred Marshall, there shone a brilliant star. As the poet spoke, the star blazed up for a second, and then slid suddenly downward across the heavens and out of sight.

They went in silently and closed the door. They found that Uncle Larry and Mr. Hobson-Cholmondeley, with two or three others, were engaged in a thorough search of the building. It

9

was a total puzzle how Fred had got out of the three rooms on the first floor, but as he was not in any one of these three rooms, it was advisable to ascertain whether or not he had left the house. The remaining members of The Full Score were in the library, and as White, Sutton and Vernon joined them, they were debating the circumstances of Fred's strange disappearance. The ghastly faces of the silent row of death-masks looked down upon them as though listening intently.

" Did you notice how uncomfortable Fred was when he saw we were only thirteen," asked Mr. J. Warren Payn.

" Who would have expected him to be superstitious ? " Vernon inquired.

" But he was—very superstitious," responded Charley Sutton; " he hated Friday.   He told me once that it was his unlucky day, and that whenever anything wrong happened to him, it was sure to be on a Friday."

" Well, to-day is Friday, isn't it ? " Mr. J. Warren Payn suggested.

" So it is ! " cried Sutton.

" Strange, indeed ! " murmured Vernon.

"It was odd, wasn't it," continued Sutton, " what he said about that fellow out in the East who hated him so; he said that if he were to die to-night mysteriously, his death would be the work of that man."

" Do you remember the man's name?" asked Vernon.

" Of course I do," replied Sutton; " I've heard Fred speak of him before. Harry Brackett and I got part of the story out of him one day last summer. His name was——"

A sharp ring of the front door bell, always audible in the library, put a stop to the discussion. Laurence Laughton and those who had been aiding him in a fruitless search of the house were coming down the stairs as the bell rang. Laughton went to the door himself. There was a moment of strained attention. Then the cheery voice of Harry Brackett was heard:

" Hello, Uncle Larry, how are you? I was afraid the boys would all be gone before I could turn up. I've had a terrible job to get interviews out of all those polyglot tramps who have come over here to sing at the Academy. I say, it's cold to-night, isn't it? There is an eager and a nipping wind, and I'll take a little nip myself."

" The feast is over, and the faithful Bridget has gone to-bed," said Uncle Larry, trying to be cheerful, despite an obstinate sinking of the heart, " but I think we can give you a bite and a sup."

Harry Brackett took a seat before the fire in the dining-room, and began an attack on the remains of the dinner. " I'm as hungry as a hunter," he said, not noting the constrained atti-

tude of his friends, "and as cold as a scientific
sermon.   And I have been working like a horse
all the afternoon.   The *City of Constantinople*,
with the whole operatic company on board, was
in dock at noon, and yet I have only just finished my story and sent it down.   I had the
devil's own luck.   First off, the manager took
me for a new deputy-sheriff, and it was three
hours before I could get at him, and I got only
a stickful when I did get it—no news, either;
of course, he promises lots of novelties, but he
let it leak out that he meant to rely on the
regular fly-blown operas we are all dead tired
of.   Next I went for the new tenor, and I've
given him a notice from Noticeville, just out of
charity, because he's the ugliest man in the
English language.   His mouth and his ears are
three sizes larger than current styles.   But here
I am, talking a straight streak."

"Go on," urged Charley Sutton; "don't mind
my feelings; keep right on."

"I do talk, and that's a fact," admitted Harry
Brackett, helping himself to a particularly
appetizing pear.   "I believe I could converse
the kick out of a mule.   A man has to be handy
with his tongue when he gets into the Apollo
House.   There's a queer den for you, all sorts
and conditions of men, women and children,
mostly show-folks.   There's a German tragedian
and a French *opéra-bouffe* troupe, and a Russian

violinist, and an Italian fakir, and—but, I say, I'm doing all the talking."

" Of course," said Eliphalet Duncan.

" And you fellows stand round and say nothing," continued Harry Brackett, "just as though something had happened."

" Something has happened," White answered.

" I thought so," Brackett declared; "you all look as serious as a conference."

" Well, I don't know," said Uncle Larry, "that it's exactly serious. But Fred Olyphant is missing. He was here a few minutes ago, and now he is gone, and we are all greatly puzzled about it."

" You don't think anything has happened to him, do you ? " asked Brackett, with interest.

" Of course," answered Eliphalet Duncan, " we have no reason to think that. But we do not know where he is."

" And we don't know how he got out of the library," added Sutton.

" We have called him, and he has not answered," Vernon said; "we have sought, and we have not found."

" That is quite queer, isn't it ?" Harry Brackett replied; "and do you think—" Then he stopped abruptly, as a new idea seemed to strike him. " Oh, I say, did Fred ever tell any of you fellows about a bad man with a black heart he met out East somewhere, a sort of a Corsican Greek with a villainous name ? "

"Do you mean Constantine Vollonides?" asked Laughton.

"Yes, that's the man. Well, he's here!" replied Harry Brackett.

"Here?" cried Charley Sutton.

"Yes, here, in New York. I suppose he arrived on the *City of Constantinople*. At all events, he's at the Apollo House. I saw the name on the register not an hour ago."

A sudden silence fell upon the little group gathered about the table in the dining-room. Laughton looked up and caught White's eyes fixed on him with an inquiring look.

Mr. Hobson-Cholmondeley was the first to speak. "*Tiens, tiens!*" he said;" it is certainly a very strange coincidence."

CHAPTER IX.

THE TOUCH OF A VANISHED HAND.

AFTER The Full Score had departed at last, Laurence Laughton passed a restless night; his mind was ill at ease and he was in love. It was not until just before dawn that he fell into a heavy and unrefreshing slumber; and it was almost noon when he was able to rouse himself and to rise. The faithful Bridget brought him his coffee and a note from Robert White. His tangled little terrier, Bundle o' Rags, sat on the chair opposite, watching him with the sharp eyes of canine affection, while he sipped his coffee and read the note. White wrote that on leaving Uncle Larry's house the night before, he had gone straight to Olyphant's studio, where he had roused the negro attendant, only to learn that the artist had not been home since the afternoon; he had called there again in the morning as he went down town, and he had received the same answer—Olyphant had not returned to his studio since he left it to go to Mrs. Sutton's tea. White suggested that if Uncle Larry would join him, it might be well to go to the artist's quarters that afternoon, and to interrogate the sable servitor more elaborately, and to see if they might not discover some sort of a clue to the mysterious disappearance of the night before.

Laughton wondered why it was that the reading of this note deepened the gloom which encompassed him about. He was depressed beyond expression. It was only with an effort that he was able to rouse himself to the performance of the routine work which demanded immediate attention. His mind kept flying away from the matter in hand; again and again he caught himself holding his pen in the air and gazing vacantly into space. Bundle o' Rags seemed to divine his need of sympathy. He followed all his master's movements with an inquiring eye and a tender solicitude to anticipate his slightest wish. Once as Larry had lost himself in an indeterminate day dream, he was brought back to consciousness by the insertion of the mop-like head of Bundle o' Rags into the left hand, which he had allowed to hang pendent by the side of the chair. The little dog thrust his head into his master's hand as though to recall his presence, and to remind him of the warm sympathy which a good dog always feels for his master. Larry patted the head of his devoted pet. " Good dog," he said, gently, " good dog ; " and Bundle o' Rags wagged his tail with an abundant joy.

Despite the companionship of the dog and the

necessity of imperative work, the day wore away slowly and painfully ; yet it drew to a close at last. For an hour or two before Robert White called for Laurence Laughton to go with him to Olyphant's studio, the avenue before Uncle Larry's door was filled with the serried ranks of a political procession, which rent the air with the shrill music of its brazen band, and with the unanimity of its oft-repeated party cries. It was the Saturday before election, and the business men of the city had turned out in force to show their faith in the candidate of the reform movement. Merchants and lawyers, tradesmen and mechanics, each grouped under the banner of his guild, marched in their thousands to prove the sincerity of their political faith. Ordinarily a sight like this—a spectacle as purely American as one could find any where or any time—would have aroused Laughton's keenest interest. But even the old war-tunes, as band after band blared them forth, failed for once to stir his blood. He was glad when a sharp ring of his door-bell told him that Robert White had come.

They shook hands in the hall.

" This is a good show," said the journalist, nodding his head toward the avenue, up which a brass band of unusual discordance was now proceeding. " We shall put our man in with a rush on Tuesday."

"Well, I don't know," Uncle Larry responded, doubtfully, with his thoughts in the air.

" I do," replied the journalist.   " Never pro-
phesy unless you know, is a good motto, but I
can almost say I do know now.   This procession
will send us up the river with a rousing majority,
and the State is safe."

With no little difficulty Laughton and White
forced their way gently through the crowds
which lined the side-walks, and which warmed
up with the enthusiasm of the paraders and sent
back answering cheers.   In a few minutes the
two men reached Fourteenth Street, and crossing
the procession they continued down Fifth
Avenue, almost as bare and deserted below as
above it had been crowded and excited.   The
day was dull and drear; and there was a chill
wind which smote them with double force, now
that they were no longer protected by the throng
of the procession and of its spectators.

Laughton and White walked along silently.
The journalist had a fancy for the solution of
puzzles, and more than once, as a volunteer, he
had cleared up mysteries which baffled the less
intelligent detectives of the regular police.   In
the present instance he felt himself at sea, with
no firm ground under his feet.   How Olyphant
could have got out of Laughton's library, and
why he should go and make no sign—these were
the problems which White was turning over and
over.   The journalist did not know how much
weight to attach to the presence in New York,

of the one deadly enemy Fred had. As yet he could not see how Constantine Vollonides could have had any hand in the artist's disappearance.

While White applied himself to these problems, with a resolute desire to solve them, he had not the strong personal interest in the solution which Laurence Laughton had: and he was able to consider them in a more favorable frame of mind. Laughton was conscious of a numbing of his faculties as he strove to concentrate them ; he was weighed down by an inexplicable dread. The melancholy of autumn had seized him, and it intensified his own dreary doubt. The reddening leaves were blown from the scant trees, and fell about his feet. At the corner of Eleventh Street, there was a misanthropic engine of torture, of the kind known as piano-organs, from which a sturdy Italian was slowly grinding forth the lugubrious strains of a ballad of temporary popularity, beseeching the hearer to wait till the clouds roll by. The trembling notes of this pitiful song emphasized Laughton's unaccountable misery. Even the sudden, sharp clang of a fire-engine, which rushed down the avenue, drawn by eager horses, urged to their utmost speed, even this, which stirs the blood of the true New Yorker upon his death-bed, failed for once to rouse Laughton from his lethargic misery.

At Tenth Street, they turned and walked toward Sixth Avenue. When they had arrived almost opposite the old Studio Building, which has harbored three generations of the painters and sculptors of New York, and just before they caught sight of the tall red bell-tower of the Jefferson-Market Court-house, the most picturesque public building of the city, they stayed their feet in front of a row of dingy little houses, two-stories high, and built of dull and faded brick. Under the high stoop of one of these desolate and most prosaic habitations, and lurking half out of sight, as though it were ashamed of itself, there was a low door. Going down two or three steps, Robert White rang the bell by the side of this unobtrusive entrance. In the distance the bell was heard to jangle harshly. White and Laughton stood on the low door-step for a minute or more, before there were any sounds of an answer to their appeal. Then a shuffling along the passage-way announced the approach of the venerable Andrew Jackson. A bolt was drawn, a key turned in a lock, and the door opened, revealing a long low passage under the house to a yard in the rear. Holding the door ajar was Andrew Jackson, a tall thin negro, with a full head of curly white hair; he had a most benevolent expression, and he spoke with an elaborate precision.

" Is that you, Mr. Laughton? Excuse me, sir, for not having been quicker to open the door, but I have my neuralgy to-day, and I am threatened with pneumony, and I cannot get about as spry as I would like to. Walk in, sir. And this is Mr. White ; walk in, sir ; walk right in." And Andrew Jackson held the door open before them, waving them in with the most graceful gestures.

" Is Mr. Olyphant at home ? " asked White.

" Not yet, sir," answered the old negro ; " not yet. But he will be 'long bimeby, he will be 'long; step in out of the cold, gentlemen." And making way for them, with a polite bow, he hastened to close the door, and to shut out the chill wind which was pouring along the damp passage. Andrew Jackson was as straight as an arrow, and as handsome as only an old negro of the better sort can be. He was very exact in his use of the English language, and the few elisions he still permitted himself seemed as though they were survivals of an earlier and ungrammatical stage of culture.

" Mr. Olyphant hasn't been home since yesterday afternoon ? " queried White.

" That is what I told you last night, sir, when you called me from my bed," replied the darkey, with dignity, and without any tone of reproach in his voice. "And that is what I told you this morning again, Mr. White. Mr. Frederick went out yesterday afternoon, and he has not yet returned. Will you walk up to the studio, gentlemen, and wait for him ? "

White and Laughton exchanged affirmative glances.

"There is a fire in the studio, gentlemen," urged the courtly negro, shivering in the chill air of the passage.

" Lead on, I'll follow thee," White declared.

Andrew Jackson conducted them through the passage into the small yard in the rear of the house.   Holding his body erect, he shuffled across this yard, which was only a few paces square, to a small oddly-shaped building which filled the end of the lot.   This building looked as though it had recently been repaired and repainted after many years of neglect and decay ; and such was the fact.   A few months before, Olyphant, in his search for a studio, happened upon this tumble-down old house on the rear of a lot.   The situation was exactly what he wished, the rent was modest, and the owner offered to pay for the repairs.   The walls were solid enough, and the roof could be made tight.   There was something bizarre about the building which fascinated Fred, and he had taken possession of it with great pleasure.   The house was tiny; the basement held a kitchen ; the ground-floor served as a sitting-room and a dining-room ; on the floor above were two little bed rooms, one for the artist and one for Andrew Jackson, who was his man-of-all work, cook, and chambermaid, messenger and model at need.   The attic floor, under a quaint gable roof, Olyphant took for his studio; he removed all the partitions, he put in enormous skylights, he enlarged the fireplaces, he had had the walls and the roof made water-proof and wind-tight; and here he worked, shut off from all extraneous distractions, as though he were at the top of a high tower, with Andrew Jackson as a jealous sentinel on guard at the foot of the stair.

The walls of the room on the ground-floor, contrived a double debt to pay, and to serve both as a dining-room and as a sitting-room, were divided into irregular rectangular panels, most of which contained pictures, studies, and sketches by Olyphant's fellow-painters. Along one side of the room was a series of battle-pieces, reminiscences of Olyphant's Russo-Turkish experience : they were cold and pitiless in their exposure of the irredeemable brutality of war. It was into this room that Andrew Jackson led Laughton and White.

"There's a fire here too, gentlemen," he said, as he held open the door for them to enter, bowing low, "and I can make a little punch for you, if you would like it, to keep out the cold?"

Laughton shook his head and White answered, "No, thank you, Andy, we are neither cold nor thirsty."

"Mr. Olyphant has some very good whiskey, sir," persisted the negro, persuasively.

"Tell me, Andy," asked White, suddenly, "is

this the first time Mr. Olyphant has been out all
night?"

"Oh, no, sir—not the first time at all. He
did not come home one night about two weeks
ago, sir."

"Two weeks ago?" intervened Laughton.
"About two weeks ago he stayed all night with
me; we were talking till very late, and he took a
bed at my house instead of going home."

"Yes, sir," Andrew Jackson corroborated,
"that is what he said when he returned. He
informed me that he had spent the night at your
residence, sir."

"And is that the only time?" continued
White.

"No, sir; I think not," Andrew Jackson
answered, trying to recollect. "In the summer,
sir, he was often away from home at night—
especially over Sunday."

"I can account for that too," Laughton declared; "he used to go to Coney Island for the
night. After I got back from Europe we ran
down together two or three times to stay over
Sunday."

"Did he notify you when he was going to be
away?" asked White.

"Sometimes he did, sir, and sometimes he
did not. He did pretty much as he happened
to feel like," replied Andrew Jackson. "He
was not very regular in his comings and

goings, sir, and there is many a good dinner I have had to eat here all alone after getting it ready for him. I expect him in soon now, sir, because to-day is Saturday, and Saturday is his reception-day. He receives in his studio the ladies and gentlemen who call. There have been two ladies here already this afternoon."

"Two ladies?" asked Laughton, surprised; "what ladies?"

"I really do not know, sir," answered Andrew Jackson. "They were young ladies, sir. One of them was very handsome, sir, with dark hair and dark eyes, and the other was smaller and younger, and she had reddish hair, sir, and it was cut short like a boy's almost—but she was quite a lady."

"That sounds like a description of Pussy Palmer," White suggested, with a smile; "but who can the other girl be?"

With the jealousy of a lover Laughton had made an instant guess at the other. But he said nothing.

"The handsome young lady called the little one 'Pussy,' sir," confirmed Andrew Jackson.

"Then it *was* the Palmer girl!" White declared, laughing; "it's just like her."

"The two ladies came together, sir, about an hour ago. They went up to the studio, and looked about for a few minutes, and then they came down here, sir, and when I asked what

10

name I should say called, the taller lady took a
rose from a big bunch she had pinned at her
waist, and she said to give that to Mr. Olyphant
when he came in and he would know who it
was.   There is the rose, sir."

A quaint Venetian ewer stood on a little table
at the window, and in this there rested a superb
yellow rose.   To Uncle Larry it seemed
strangely like the yellow roses which he had
seen fastened to the girdle of Winifred Marshall
the afternoon before.   But perhaps this was
fancy, he said to himself; there is more than one
tall, handsome, dark-haired girl in New York,
and there are yellow roses in plenty.

" Shall we go up stairs? " asked White, and
Laughton waked from his day-dream and
assented.

Andrew Jackson, despite the rheumatism which
twisted his long legs, preceded them briskly,
and yet with dignity, up the little stairs ·leading
to the attic.   The studio occupied the whole top
of the house, and it was none too large.   The
stairs came up in one corner unexpectedly and
with a certain picturesque abruptness.   In the
large fire-place which dominated the room, there
sparkled and crackled a comfortable fire which had
taken the chill from the air.   The dull and fading
light of a dreary autumn afternoon came in, gray
and cold, through the broad sky-lights.   Antique
cabinets and curious old presses were filled with

a heterogeny of costumes; and other costumes in tumultuous abundance were visible through the half-opened door of a closet. There were three or four tables of varying design and age; and no two of the chairs were alike; they were all studio properties bought one at a time, to serve the special purpose of a picture. Against the walls were dozens of huge portfolios filled with photographs and engravings and studies. Two easels held pictures partly finished. On one was the 'Sharpness of Death,' the work to which Olyphant had been giving his best thought for the past few months. On the other was a canvas concealed by a cloth thrown carefully over it. A chair near this was littered with brushes, tubes of paint, bits of charcoal and what not. Around the studio, here and there, against the wall, or leaning upon a table, were canvases of all sizes,—bits of color, "effects" seized and set down at the moment, anatomical studies, careful copies from life, side by side with faces which were expression only, as they were almost without features. Nowhere was there anything flashy or facile or meretricious; there was no *chic* to be seen; there was no mere reveling in manual cleverness; there were rather the evidences of the hard work of an honest workman, toiling as best he knew how to overcome and to conquer a rebel material, and to force the erring hand to do the bidding of the brain.

Upon its side on a settee reclined a lay-figure swathed in Oriental draperies richly embroidered. A dagger was thrust into the figure behind the shoulder, as though its point were meant for the heart.

Laughton had given himself up to the pathos of the deserted studio, when White touched him and pointed to the murdered lay-figure.

"That is a startling thing for us to see just now, isn't it?" asked the journalist.

"Yes, sir," replied Andrew Jackson, before Laughton had roused himself to respond; "it frightened the young ladies a good deal. The little one with the hair cut short shrieked right out, but the other one went up to it at once."

"Did the two young ladies come up here?" Laughton asked.

"Oh, yes, sir," answered Andrew Jackson. "When Mr. Olyphant is not in, I always show the studio to ladies. They were very much interested, sir, very much."

"You say one of the young ladies was not frightened at this assassination here?" White asked; "I wonder who it was."

Laughton gave White a sharp glance as though to share in any guess he might make.

Andrew Jackson straightened a fold in the drapery of the lay-figure, and continued, "No, sir, she was not afraid at all. She came over here to it, and she put her hand on the dagger,—

so—and just then I heard something drop. I thought it sounded like a ring, but the young lady said it was a cat's eye." Here Andrew Jackson smiled a smile of conscious knowledge. "Of course, sir, I knew better than that. I knew that if a cat let her eye fall on the floor it would not make a noise like a gold ring. I thought the young lady wanted to have some fun, perhaps; and so, sir, I said nothing; nothing at all !"

" Did she show you the cat's-eye ? " Laughton asked.

"Oh, no, sir," answered Andrew Jackson, smiling again as sagely as before; "she did not show it to me. She told the other young lady that she was very glad to have found it."

Laughton was standing near the easel holding the covered canvas. He stepped forward impatiently and, with an effort, he asked, " What was this young lady like ? "

White looked at him in surprise.

Andrew Jackson answered, "I told you, sir, already, she was a very handsome young lady, tall and—" Here Andrew Jackson happened to look up, and his eyes fell on the picture on the easel, from which Laughton's impatient movement had shaken the cover. " Why, there, sir," cried the negro, " there's a portrait of the young lady, sir, quite as good as a photograph."

On the canvas from which the curtain had fallen thus opportunely, there were only a few bold, rapid strokes in charcoal, outlining a female head.

" Why, it is Miss Marshall ! " White cried.

" Do you think so ? " asked Laughton, facing him, sternly.

" Yes," answered White, gazing at the portrait again, " or, at any rate, it is strangely like her. That head alone," he continued, enthusiastically, " would be enough to prove the genius of Frederick Olyphant. See how he has seen into the girl's soul, and how he has set down the spiritual essence of her character in a few touches of black-and-white.   It is marvelous."

Laurence Laughton looked at the picture intently. It was Winifred Marshall beyond a doubt—Winifred Marshall without the veil of haunting melancholy which was wont to shroud her face ; Winifred Marshall with the light of love in her eyes. Sick at heart, Laughton lifted the cloth and covered the canvas again with care.   Then he said, "Let's be going ; we have discovered nothing as yet."

As they passed down stairs and out into the yard, White sighed and said : " Well, I confess I am disappointed. I had hoped that we might find some clue to Fred's fate."

" What, sir," asked Andrew Jackson, seizing White's arm in his right hand and talking with great excitement, "you didn't think nothing has happen to Mas'r Frederick, do you, sah?"

"We do not know," White answered, gently. "We are trying to find out what has become of him."

"Then he ain't a-comin' back bimeby? An' that's why you've been askin' questions? Poor Mas'r Frederick! Poor Mas'r Frederick" And the faithful servant had to make an effort to keep back the sobs that rose to his throat.

"Do you know anybody who has a grudge .against Mr. Olyphant?" White inquired, when they stood once more in the street.

"No, sah; Mas'r Frederick never hurted no one, sah; I know that, sah," answered the poor negro, with all his precision of speech and all his pride of manner gone from him. "And there ain't no suspicious characters been about here, neither. I don't believe Mas'r Frederick ever laid eyes on a Voodoo woman."

White could not keep back a smile, but to hide it from the devoted negro, he said, "So there have been no suspicious characters about here?"

"No, sah, none. That is, sah, not to-day, sah."

"Was there a suspicious character here yesterday?" asked White, hastily.

"Well, sah, I don't know, sah. But yesterday afternoon, just after Mas'r Frederick go, sah, I was out here, polishing the door-knob, sah, and a strange man came by, and he stopped, and he asked me if Mas'r Frederick Olyphant lived here, and I said he did, but he had just gone. Then the strange man went right down the street after Mas'r Fred."

"This was yesterday afternoon?" White asked.

"Yes, sir; yesterday afternoon about three or four o'clock," answered Andrew Jackson.

White hesitated a moment, then he inquired:

"Why do you call this strange man a suspicious character?"

In his turn Andrew Jackson hesitated. At last he answered: "He gave me a gold dollar not to tell any one he had called. And you are the first one I have told at all."

"He gave you a gold dollar?" Laughton asked, in sharp surprise.

"Yes, sir."

"What was he like?"

"He was a peculiar-looking man, sir, although he was dressed like a perfect gentleman. I noticed his boots, and he had very small feet. I misdoubt he was a stranger—a foreigner."

"Why?"

"Because he had a queer accent. He spoke English nearly as well as we do, sir," and Andrew Jackson made a polite bow; "but he had a queer accent—very queer."

"Was he a Frenchman?"

"Oh, no, sir. No, he was not a Frenchman.

I speak French myself—that is, I speak it a little
—and I know he was not a Frenchman. And
he did not seem like a German. Perhaps, sir.
he was an I-talian."

"An Italian?" repeated Laughton, mechani-
cally, as he and White exchanged a meaning
glance. "Had he any other peculiarity?"

"No, sir; no—except his white face,—that
was very white, sir, very white indeed."

"Was there a scar in the centre of the forehead?" asked Laughton, quickly.

"How did you know that, sir," said Andrew
Jackson, taken aback.

"Did he have a scar there? Yes or no?"

"Oh, yes, sir; he did—at least I thought I saw
a scar there, but he had a hat on and—"

"Had he a dark mustache?"

"Yes, sir—a black mustache?"

"That is the man!" said Laughton to White.

"Constantine Vollonides?" White asked.

"Constantine Vollonides," answered Laughton.

They left Andrew Jackson standing with dignity before the underground passage to Olyphant's
studio, and they walked rapidly to the Apollo
House, where Harry Brackett had seen the
name of Constantine Vollonides on the register.
By this time darkness had fallen on the city, but
at Fifth Avenue and Fourteenth Street, the
political procession was still passing, and the air
was filled with the martial strains of the John

Brown march. Hurriedly crossing to Union Square, Laughton and White made their way at once to the Apollo House, which was only a stone's throw beyond.

They went to the office and asked the clerk, "Is Mr. Constantine Vollonides staying here?"

"He has gone," the clerk answered, with the curtness which is the chief characteristic of the hotel clerk.

"When?"

"Last night."

"At what time?"

The clerk called across the hall to a porter, "Pete, what time last night did the gent in 47 go?"

Pete replied promptly, "He come in a little after eleven, and I got him a coupé, and he went up to the Grand Central to catch the midnight train for Chicago."

As Laughton and White came out of the hotel, the latter asked, "What time was it when you missed Fred last night?"

"A little after ten, I think."

White whistled meditatively. "And Constantine Vollonides did not return to the hotel till after eleven," he said.

CHAPTER X.

THE RETURN OF DEAR JONES.

THE next day was Sunday, and Frederick Olyphant had last been seen on Friday evening; for nearly forty-eight hours he had not been heard from. A certain aroma of eccentricity clung about the artist, and some of his friends thought it perfectly possible that he had all at once taken the freak of going off by himself, to get away from the turmoil and the worry of the city. Possible, this might be, but probable it was not. As Bob White summed up the situation, there were three problems to solve : First, how had Fred got out of Uncle Larry's library? second, why had he gone without warning? and, third, where was he now? The presence of Constantine Vollonides in New York, his inquiry at the artist's studio, and his sudden departure from town, shortly after Olyphant's disappearance, these were all circumstances which complicated the situation not a little. They might be significant, and again they might be only fortuitous coincidences.

When Monday morning came and brought no

news, Robert White went to Laurence Laughton, and suggested that the time had come to call on the police, and to get what aid they might give. Laurence was anxious not to arouse public speculation, knowing how unpleasant all notoriety would be to the artist were he to return as suddenly as he had gone. But White convinced him that to inform the proper authorities was a duty they had no right to postpone any longer, and he yielded at last, although still unwilling. They went together to police headquarters, which they found in a high state of activity, as the morrow would be election day, when a double responsibility is imposed on the police of New York. In the course of his work on the *Gotham Gazette*, Robert White had had occasion to meet Inspector Barnes, the head of the detective force, and he knew him to be courteous, prompt, active, and full of resource. To Inspector Barnes, therefore, he sent up his card, and despite the pressure of work, he and Laughton were invited at once into the private office of the inspector, who received them cordially.

" What can I do for you to-day, gentlemen ? " asked the inspector, lighting a fresh cigar.

Robert White made a plain statement of the case. Inspector Barnes listened attentively, smoking in silence and never interrupting except to put a pertinent question at the apt moment. When the story was told he meditated a minute

or two. Then he took up a pen and made a few
notes. He asked for a full description of the
missing man, and said that he would have the
general alarm sent out at once, and that the
whole force of the police would thereafter be on
the lookout. He added that he doubted whether
there was any need to be excited, as in all pro-
bability Mr. Olyphant would soon reappear all
right, and with a valid reason for his absence.
In view of this fortunate contingency, Laughton begged that as little publicity as possible be
given to the disappearance. As they were
making ready to leave the inspector to his work,
he asked again about Laurence's library, and
.about the means of egress from it. Laughton
made a sketch-plan of his ground-floor, and the
inspector jotted a few more notes on the back
of this and put it away in a drawer. Then he
inquired whether Mr. Olyphant was likely to
have had any money or valuables on his person,
and also whether he was known fo have any
enemies. Thus interrogated, Laughton sat
down again and told the inspector about Constantine Vollonides, setting forth the grounds of
the quarrel at Perà, the threat of the Greek that
the next meeting should have a different ending,
and his arrival in New York a few hours before
Olyphant's strange disappearance. The inspector
listened attentively, and asked if the Greek was
still in New York. " It will do no harm to

have him watched," he remarked, when he was informed that Constantine Vollonides had left the city for Chicago on the midnight train of Friday. " First of all, we must find out whether he really took that train or not. You may rely on me to attend to that."

Again White and Laughton arose to go, thanking the inspector for his courtesy.

" One word more, gentlemen," said he, as they reached the door, " Is there a woman in the case."

Instantly White and Laughton replied together, " No."

" Indeed ? " returned Inspector Barnes. " That complicates matters a little." Then he held the door open for them and they passed out. When they had gone, he touched a bell, and he gave instructions to the officer who responded to the summons to go to the Apollo House and to find the driver of the carriage which took Constantine Vollonides to the Grand Central Depot on Friday night, and to ascertain whether or not the Greek had taken the midnight train ; and if he had, to discover when and where he had left the train ; whether at Chicago or at some point short of Chicago.

A day passed, and two days and three days, and the friendly prediction of Inspector Barnes was not realized : Frederick Olyphant did not reappear. A President of the United States was

elected on Tuesday; and for several days thereafter there was some slight doubt as to the
result of the vote. For a little while the most
intense excitement prevailed throughout the
nation, and the newspapers had no space to spare
for an incident so unimportant comparatively as
the disappearance of one man. Toward the end
of the week public opinion began to settle, and
in the minds of even the most violent political
partisans, doubt gave way slowly to the assur-
ance of defeat or of victory. But the sickening
uncertainty of Olyphant's fate was not resolved
away by any definite news. Some of his friends
felt that they would rather be told positively of
his death than remain in the intolerable doubt
into which the mystery of his vanishing had
plunged them.

Laurence Laughton opened his newspaper
every morning in fear and trembling. He
dreaded to see an imaginative account of Frederick's disappearance spread through two or
three columns, with an abundance of needless
detail, vulgar and personal. Fortunately, the
newspapers found metal more attractive to their
readers in the description of the final throes of
the political trouble. And so the dull days
dragged on, and he had only the " no news "
which is never " good news." At last a full
week had passed; it was again Friday, just seven
days since The Full Score had met at his house

to dine; and he had promised to go to dinner at
Mrs. Martin's.

The Duchess of Washington Square had
always been very fond of Miss Phyllis Van
Renssellaer; she it was who had introduced
Dear Jones to her, and she had been a party to
his ardent courtship. She rejoiced at their marriage and sent them a pair of beautiful silver lamps
as a wedding present. And now when Mr.
and Mrs. Delancey Jones returned on the
City of Constantinople from their summer
wedding-trip in Europe, Mrs. Martin made haste
to give them a dinner. As a matter of course,
Laurence Laughton was the first one to be
invited. The Duchess of Washington Square
could not give a dinner to Dear Jones and Baby
Van Renssellaer and not ask their best friend,
Uncle Larry. It was almost as much a matter
of course that Miss Winifred Marshall should be
the next on the list, for the close intimacy of
Miss Van Renssellaer and Miss Marshall was
well known to the Duchess. Indeed, if it had
not been for the certainty that he should see
Winifred, Laurence would have excused himself
from the dinner; he was in no mood for the very
small talk and idle babble which is bandied about
briskly at a fashionable dinner. Ordinarily he
was an expert at this conversational battledore
and shuttle-cock, but he had no mind now for
frivolity and froth. He was too fond of Olyphant

not to take his fate to heart, and until the doubt was resolved Laurence was not in the vein for chaff and chatter. Yet to sit beside Winifred for an hour or two, or even to be able to gaze upon her across the table, to feast his eyes with a sight of the woman he loved—this was a felicity he had not strength to forego. And he did not regret that he had mastered his repugnance when he saw that good fortune and the Duchess of Washington Square had decided that he should take in to dinner Miss Winifred Marshall.

She greeted him cordially as though she were indeed glad to see him; there was a heartiness in her welcome which he had never before noted since love had sharpened his eyes to spy out even the smallest sign. She was as superbly beautiful as ever, despite the dark lines under the eyes, telling of loss of sleep, and despite the look of doubt and anxiety which lurked upon her face. His heart beat high as he offered her his arm. She took it with a confiding gesture, as though she expected counsel or comfort from him. During the dinner he noted that to him at least she revealed none of the haughtiness which he had considered one of her chief characteristics, and which he had even thought to accord aptly with her splendid beauty. She listened to him with deference; and to him she was all gentleness. She was a tamed bird, and Laurence wondered what had wrought the change.

Twice or thrice he caught her eyes fixed on him with a questioning gaze, as though she were trying to make up her mind. After he had talked to her for an hour, he began to resent her attitude toward him; it was too confiding; in a word, too filial. Now, his love for her was not paternal. He was twice her age, he knew, but at forty he felt himself a young man still. He rebelled against a confidence which seemed to say that he was too old for a girl to need to be on her guard. This feeling of resentment almost betrayed him into harsh and hasty words, which he luckily cut short as they came to the tip of his tongue. Then, as he looked in her face and saw the loneliness and the melancholy which were always to be seen there, now intensified and accentuated by doubt and dread, he felt a sudden pang of poignant self-reproach. He was moved almost to ask if he could not be of service to her, and to bid her command him, for she had the right; he was her faithful servant forever, and it was a joy for him to be at her beck and call, for he loved her. But at the dinner-table, with neighbors next to them on each side and near to them opposite, there was no fit occasion to speak. They talked about trifles and laughed sadly about nothing. Twice, when there was an animated conversation going on all around them, she leaned forward and made ready to say something to him, which apparently she did not wish

to be heard by the others. As it happened there
was an accidental lull in the political discussion
which had been raging, and the young statesmen
about the dinner-table stopped fighting their battles
o'er and turned their attention first to the Roman
punch and then to the canvas-backs. The same
ill-fortune pursued them after dinner. Twice again
Winifred manœuvred skillfully to get Uncle
Larry where she could have a moment's personal
converse with him, and twice her innocent scheme
was frustrated by accident. The first time was
shortly after dinner, and then Mr. Hobson-Cholmondeley joined them at once and began to compliment Miss Marshall on her dress. Before
Pussy Palmer could capture him and lead him
away, a little group had formed about them. The
second time was just before the gathering was
about to break up; and then it was Mrs. Jones
who bore down upon them.

"Uncle Larry, I haven't had a chance to talk
to Winifred all the evening. I mean to take her
home in my cab. You and Lance can walk up
together!"

Against this peremptory mandate no protest
would have been availing. Uncle Larry bowed
low and said:

"Your Majesty's lightest wish is to me a law!"

And then Mrs. Jones bore Winifred away that
they might perform the mysterious rite known
to women as "putting on their things."

When they reappeared, duly apparelled, Dear Jones cried :

" Phyllis, you are not going out without something on your head ? "

" Indeed I am," answered the bride; " I don't need anything. I'm not light-headed and I shan't blow away."

Already Dear Jones knew that remonstrance was useless. He sighed sarcastically. " Uncle Larry," he said, "you see how well she loves, honors and obeys."

Then he took Winifred down the steps and put her into the cab, while Laughton escorted Mrs. Jones and ensconced her by the side of Miss Marshall. As the cab drove off the bride called back to them :

" Uncle Larry, don't keep Lance up late. It isn't good for his health ! "

" Do you hear that ? " said Dear Jones to Uncle Larry; " I'm under petticoat government already."

" You seem to thrive under it," retorted Laurence, as they turned into Fifth Avenue and began to walk up briskly against a shrill-tongued wind which made them button their overcoats tightly across. " A strong government is good for you; and what you need is one-woman power."

" Then I've got what I need," answered Jones. " I kiss my chains, of course, and I adore my jailer; but I am bound hand and foot."

"Well, I don't know," said Uncle Larry; "I suppose you can get a divorce in Indiana or Connecticut if she treats you cruelly."

"It's the most delicious cruelty in the world, Uncle Larry—no home is complete without it."

"If you have a home already," Laughton declared, "you must have been pretty quick about it."

"I was quick—and I have a home. It is a flat, up at the top of a huge house, overlooking Central Park—take the elevator. We have a tiny little parlor, and a tiny little library, and a tiny little kitchen, and a tiny little dining-room, where we hope soon to give Uncle Larry a tiny little dinner. I have grand prospects now—I can see all over the Park. I have the first floor counting from the roof down—it's a sky-parlor, excellently adapted for astronomical research. Altogether it is the most delightful little den you ever saw, although there isn't room enough in the whole apartment to swing a mouse, let alone a cat, did I desire to indulge in that feline amusement."

"I'm glad you are happy, my boy," said Uncle Larry, with a sigh.

"Why not?" replied Dear Jones. "Isn't everybody happy now? My malison on the man who dares to be miserable! I'll none of him."

As they passed Tenth Street, Jones happened

to think of Olyphant, and he asked Laughton how it was that he had not met the painter since his return.

" Don't you know he has not been seen since a week ago to-night?" Laurence asked, in astonishment.

" No," answered Dear Jones, " I know nothing at all. I am newly married. I am just back from Europe, and I have just found, furnished and moved into a flat. I have heard that a President of these United States was elected this week. But further than this I am absolutely ignorant. Tell me all about it."

Before Laughton could tell him the half of the tale they had arrived before Uncle Larry's door.

" Come in for a few minutes," he said to Jones, " and smoke a cigar, and I will give you the rest of the story on the spot."

" You can have me for twenty minutes precisely," remarked Dear Jones, as he looked at his watch while Uncle Larry was opening the door. " I have not been home later than midnight as yet, and I don't want to spoil my record."

They walked into the library, and Laughton lighted the gas. Jones looked up at the cornice and saw the silent row of death-masks standing out in lurid relief.

" Ugh !" he groaned with a shiver ; " we are

down among the dead men here with a
vengeance. This is just the place for a tale of
mystery. Have you such a thing as an *oubliette*
in the house ? "

" You don't think I killed him, do you ? "
asked Laughton, with sudden savageness.

"Why not ? " Jones replied, laughing. " Perhaps you have him concealed somewhere about
the premises, in solitary confinement—in the
cellar, for instance."

Laughton listened to this ill-timed levity with
ill-concealed impatience. " Shall I tell you about
it or not ? " he asked, abruptly.

" Fire away," answered Jones, helping himself
to one of Uncle Larry's little cigars from a bunch
which filled a cup of Japanese *cloisonné* on the
mantlepiece.

Jones leaned back in an easy chair; and
Laughton began walking up and down the room,
as he set forth the circumstance of Olyphant's
last day in New York. When he came to the
search for the artist and the absolute impossibility
of finding any clue to his fate, Jones started up
and said :

" I say, Uncle Larry, this is serious. Now,
just stop prowling up and down like a bear in a
cage, or a peripatetic philosopher, and tell me
again just how it was that he went."

" To sum up in as few words as possible,"
answered Laurence, " he was standing on this

rug here as I am now, and he suddenly disappeared."

"He vanished and made no sign, just as though he had been sitting on Aladdin's carpet, but the carpet is still here, and the man is gone. It is odd."

"Odd?" replied Laughton, impatiently; "odd? It is absolutely incomprehensible."

"That's what I said," replied Jones; "it is very odd indeed. One thing is certain, he is gone. Now, I don't believe, all things considered, that he went willingly."

"Well, I don't know," said Uncle Larry, dubiously; "why should he go?"

"I know reasons why he shouldn't," answered Jones.

Laughton looked at him for a moment intently, but said nothing.

"And if he did not go willingly," Jones continued, "there's a bold, bad man at the bottom of it. Now, whom do you suspect?"

"Circumstances seem to point to a Greek, named Constantine Vollonides, who—"

"What?" interrupted Jones, "a man with a scar on his forehead like a black heart?"

"Do you know him?" Larry asked, in astonishment.

"Why not?" answered Jones. "Didn't he cross with me in the *City of Constantinople* a week ago? And now I come to think of it, didn't he try to pump me about Fred?"

It was Uncle Larry's turn to ask for information.

" I'll tell you all I know," said Dear Jones. " I met the man in the smoking-room. He was a white-faced fellow; indeed, he had the whitest face of any man I ever saw. He had a thin black mustache and a little imperial, and piercing black eyes; in fact, if it had not been for the scar on his forehead, I should say he looked just like Edwin Booth, as *Iago*."

" That is the man," Laughton declared.

" He seemed a good enough sort of a fellow," continued Dear Jones, " and I thought he took a fancy to me. He lost a bet on the run the first day and another the next day; of course, I didn't trust him: I fear the Greeks even bearing gifts. But he stuck to me and we let him into a little game of poker, with which we filled up the long afternoon. And I half suspected that he let me win. Then, as we got nearer to New York, he began to ask all sorts of questions about America and the people here. I remember I mentioned you, and he said he had met you in the East during the war, with a friend of yours, an artist, Mr. Oripant. I said ' Frederick Olyphant?' and he said, yes, he thought Olyphant was the name. And then he asked me about Fred, casually, of course, but pertinaciously. I see now that he was pumping me. Luckily I did not let out much, though I believe I did tell him about the engagement." .

"What engagement?" asked Laughton, in a hard voice, and with a sudden chill at his heart, as he stopped short in his walk and stood before Jones.

"Why, Fred's, of course. Don't you know?"

"No, I do not know."

"Oh, I forgot it was a secret. You must keep it, or I shall get well scolded."

"I can keep a secret," said Uncle Larry, slowly.

"Well, you see, Phyllis and Winifred were always great friends, and when Winifred was engaged, just like a girl, she felt she must tell somebody, so she wrote it over to Phyllis under a solemn pledge of secresy, and Phyllis got the letter just before we sailed, and she told me in strict confidence, as between man and wife. And I was just fool enough to let it out to the Greek."

"Do you mean to tell me that Frederick Olyphant was engaged to be married to Winifred?" asked Laurence Laughton, slowly, and with an effort to swallow a lump in his throat.

"Yes; but it's a dead secret, remember; you mustn't let it out as I have done!"

Laughton sat down silently and stared before him at the empty fireplace. He did not hear the clock strike.

Dear Jones jumped up. "Half-past eleven?" he cried; "my time has come. The henpecked bridegroom must be up and away. So-long,

Uncle Larry,—see you later." As they passed
into the hall, Jones turned to Laughton, and said,
with feeling, " Don't think me heartless, Uncle
Larry, because I am lively and flippant. I trust
nothing has happened to Fred—and for the present I refuse to believe that there is really any
cause for anxiety ; he will turn up all right, never
fear! But if I can do anything to help in the
search for him, call on me and I shall be on deck
at once."

Laurence Laughton went to the door with
Jones and saw him depart. Then he locked and
bolted the door, and put out the gas on the
ground-floor. He did this regular nightly work
with a dull mechanical precision, going about it
with fixed and staring eyes, like a man walking
in his sleep. He went up to his own room and
threw himself on the bed, and buried his face in
the pillow. He was not a weakling, to weep, but
the contact of the cool linen was refreshing to
his throbbing head and to his dry and burning
eye-lids. There was an utter physical abandon-
ment in his prone position. He knew the worst
now. He had hardly hoped for himself; he had
suspected that there was another ; he had
doubted whether that other was the missing man
or not. Now, he knew. Winifred loved Fred—
and they were betrothed. This it was that
Fred could not tell him when they talked just
before they parted. This was the meaning of

her visit to his studio on the Saturday afternoon; and this was the secret of the single yellow rose she had left as a token of love. Laurence was glad she had chosen Fred, for he was worthy of her: he would make her happy since she had set her heart on him: he was a noble fellow, and they were well mated. Laurence wished that Fred were standing before him that he might give him his good wishes and bid him live for her and make her happy. He could master his own misery, he hoped, if only he knew that she were happy. Men had loved before him, and had lost; and, after all, Fred was more worthy of her. Then, all at once, he remembered that Fred was not before him, that he was gone, no one knew where or how, that for ought any one could tell, he might be dead. Dead? The dreadful word rang in his brain. Dead? And if Fred were dead, why then——? Then in time perhaps Winifred might forget him. If Fred had disappeared finally and forever, in time, perhaps, there might be a chance for another to win her.

Laurence Laughton put these selfish thoughts from him resolutely and at once. He arose and began again to pace the floor. For Winifred's sake, he said to himself, the mystery of Fred's fate must be cleared up. For her sake, there must be certainty. Fredrick Olyphant must be found—alive or dead. For her sake, Laurence Laughton hoped that he might be found alive and well. And he promised himself that he would not give over the quest until he had fathomed the mystery.

He paused in his walk and stood for a moment at the window, looking out into the black night. From a dark corner of the room, Bundle o' Rags had been watching his master, and the little dog judged that the time had now come to offer sympathy; so he came forward gently and jumped into the chair by his master's side and thrust his hairy little head into the palm of his master's hand. And immediately Uncle Larry felt comforted by the thought that he had faithful friends.

CHAPTER XI.

CERTAIN of the New York newspapers are accustomed to publish on Sunday a special column devoted to a consideration of What is Going on in Society; it is an impertinent and an offensive custom, borrowed perhaps from the London weekly papers, which thrive on the retailing of petty gossip about lords and ladies. On the Sunday after Mrs. Martin's dinner to Mr. and Mrs. Delancey Jones, which was the second Sunday since the meeting of The Full Score, there appeared in one of these articles a paragraph, setting forth, in the forcible-feeble style which the writers of such stuff are wont to affect, that much interest had been aroused in society by the remarkable rumors now flying about town anent the extraordinary disappearance of a very promising young artist, who had been the hero of the most romantic adventures in the East, and whose pictures had been greatly admired at the last exhibition of the Royal Academy in London and at the last Salon in Paris. The writer of the paragraph kindly gave the missing man a certifi-

cate of good character, by adding that the gos-
sips were at a loss to suggest a reason for his
sudden flight, as no scandal had hitherto been
attached to his name.

The allusion to Frederick Olyphant was
unmistakable, and it made hopeless any attempt
to keep the matter out of the papers. On the
Monday morning, and for several mornings
thereafter, the first place in the newspapers of
New York was given up to a statement of
the circumstances of Olyphant's disappearance.
Every detail which could be gleaned by the most
industrious of reporters, or invented by the most
imaginative, was laid before the readers of the
newspapers, with a luxury of alluring and alliterative head-lines. A little evening paper called
the *Comet* surpassed itself and broke the record :
under the familiar heading " Frederick's Freak ;"
and accompanied by a portrait of the artist and
an outline sketch of the incomplete picture, 'The
Sharpness of Death,' it gave a most circumstan-
tial account of Olyphant's departure for Europe,
in company with an unknown lady supposed to
be the wife of a distinguished member of the
diplomatic corps at Washington. The other
newspapers had no difficulty in showing that the
artist had not sailed for Europe on the steamer
indicated, and that no member of the diplomatic
corps at Washington had lost a wife—not even
the Turkish minister, who had several, and could

have spared one with less inconvenience than his colleagues. The *Comet* corrected these unimportant details, and re-affirmed the substantial accuracy of its story, which it strengthened by the publication of a second portrait of Olyphant, a little less like him even than the first. As Dear Jones said, if the artist were as ugly in body and mind as these portraits represented him to be, he was fully justified in committing suicide and in escaping from his misery as soon as might be.

In an obscure corner of the *Gotham Gazette* of Wednesday, there was a short paragraph which read as follows :—

"*Found Floating in the Bay.*—A tangled mass of seaweed, floating with the tide, caught the attention of little Oscar Brautigam at a dock at Fort Hamilton yesterday morning. Mixed with the seaweed was a tuft of human hair. The bright little boy shouted for assistance, and in a few minutes those who came at his call drew from the watery seaweed the dead body of a man. The body had been in the water nearly a week, as far as could be judged by appearances. It was clothed in a well-made suit of clothes, the work of Goole & Co., the London tailors. A handsome gold watch and a heavy gold chain was found on the person of the deceased, together with a knife, and a pocket-book containing nearly twenty dollars. There were no papers by which the remains could be identified nor was the under-linen marked. The body was that of a man between thirty and forty. There were no marks to indicate that the man had met with violence. It is supposed that he committed suicide. The body was taken in charge by Coroner Stennett, of Bay Ridge, who will hold an inquest to-day."

In the course of a twelvemonth the dark waters of New York Bay cover many a crime and hide many a secret; not always do they give up their dead; and yet the finding of a floating body is common enough to call forth no special attention. It happened however that the paragraph above was read by Harry Brackett. " Read your own paper," was the first of the rules by which the staff of the *Gotham Gazette* was governed. Harry Brackett read his own paper; he saw this paragraph, and he started at once for Bay Ridge. It had struck him that an examination of this dead man and of his effects might solve the mystery of Olyphant's fate.

When he arrived at Bay Ridge, he sought out Coroner Stennett, whom he knew of old, and with whom he maintained pleasant relations, as was his duty as a reporter. He got sight of the body, but he found, as he had expected, that from long exposure it was beyond recognition. All that he could say with certainty was that the dead man was not unlike Olyphant, and that it was quite possible that this was the body

12

of Olyphant.   He examined the clothes on the
body, and he noted the name of the tailor   He
discovered that the collar of the coat was torn as
though in a struggle, and he thought he could
see on the body certain slight marks of blows.
These might have been inflicted since death, but
Harry Brackett thought not.   He asked to see
the pocket-book, but he found nothing in this of
any significance, save a cutting from the *Gotham
Gazette*, printed on the morning of election day ;
the Tuesday of the week before and four days
after Olyphant had disappeared.   If therefore the
body was that of the artist, he had lived four days
after the Friday night dinner of The Full Score.
Then the Coroner showed him the watch and
chain.   The watch bore the monogram " F. O."
or " O. F.," surmounted by an inscription in
Oriental characters.   Harry Brackett tore a thin
sheet of paper from his note-book, and took a
rubbing of the side of the watch case.   Then he
examined the watch-chain, which had not been
wholly cleansed from the seaweed twisted about
it in the water.   When he had removed this, he
made a discovery.   At the end of the chain there
was a golden claw, like a vulture's, clutching in its
talons a leaden bullet.   As Harry Brackett was
examining this singular charm, the link parted
which had bound it to the chain, and the claw
remained in his hand.

Late that afternoon, as Laurence Laughton

was gazing vacantly out of his window at a first slight and premature flurry of snow which was obscuring the glory of the November sunset, there came a sudden ring at his door. A few seconds later, Harry Brackett was ushered into the parlor. By the expression on his face, Laughton knew he had news.

"You have heard something," he cried, striding across the room and grasping Brackett by the hand; "speak, man! Out with it!"

"Don't tire yourself by being too hasty," answered the reporter, who, despite his deep interest in Olyphant, could never free himself from a constitutional levity of manner. "There was a man once died in a hurry, and he never ceased to regret it."

"Tell me—"

"Let's begin at the beginning," interrupted Brackett, "that'll save time. Read this paragraph." And he handed the newspaper which described the finding of the body at Fort Hamilton.

"Surely you do not think that this is Fred?" asked Laughton.

"Well, now, Uncle Larry, you hold your horses. I'm not going to say what I think; I'll give you facts, solid facts."

"Go on, then, in your own way," said Larry, wearily.

Brackett sat down on the piano-stool and began:

"As soon as I read that paragraph I made a straight streak for Bay Ridge. I know Coroner Stennett; we used to go to school together in Brooklyn. He took me right in to see the remains. They are unrecognizable—"

"Then what makes you think that Fred—" Laughton began again. He checked himself, as Brackett raised his hand, and said, " Tell me all you know as soon as you can."

"Who was Fred's tailor?" asked the reporter.

"Well, I don't know," said Uncle Larry, "I think he got his things in London, but I don't remember the name—"

"What is Goole & Co.?" Brackett inquired.

"Goole & Co.—that's the name," answered Laurence ; "why—"

"The clothes found on the body were made by Goole & Co."

Laughton sighed gently. " Go on," he said.

"Did you ever see his watch?" Brackett asked.

"Often."

"Was it marked?"

"Yes."

"How?"

"It had his monogram, F. O., with an inscription in Arabic, meaning Allah is good, and praying him to guard the possessor of the watch. It was given to him by an old Turkish merchant, whose life he had saved during the war."

"Would you recognize it?" asked Brackett.

" Yes."

The reporter laid before Uncle Larry the thin slip of paper on which he had made a rubbing of the side of the watch-case. Laughton knew it as soon as he saw it.

" Yes," he said, " that is his watch."

" It was found on the body," continued the reporter, " and at the end of the watch-chain was this." And he opened his hand, and on the palm of it lay the golden vulture's claw, grasping the bullet of lead.

Laughton looked at it earnestly ; he had seen it often before ; he knew how superstitiously Olyphant clung to it ; and he saw the full significance of its presence in his house under the sad circumstances. " So there's an end," he said, softly to himself, and for the first time since his friend had gone, he gave up the hope of seeing him again, alive and in the flesh.

" Your are too previous, Uncle Larry," responded the reporter, who had caught Laughton's words, " altogether too previous. So was I. It seemed to me a pretty clear case, and I thought The Full Score would have to order a rosewood casket, and a silver plate engraved with Frederick Olyphant's name. I confess I thought there couldn't be any doubt, and— "

" How can there be any now ? " interrupted Laughton, with a look at the golden claw with its leaden bullet as it lay on the table.

"It's lucky I went to the office before coming up here. I had a talk with Bob White; he writes brevier now, but he doesn't put on any more airs, and we get on first rate. I told him what I've told you, and I showed him what I've showed you. First thing he asked was, whether I was dead sure that this was Fred's body."

"Well?"

"Well, I had to tell him that of course I wasn't sure, but I hadn't any doubts. Then he asked me if this body had the scar of a bullet-wound in the left arm just by the elbow. Do you remember that Fred had been wounded there?"

"He had," answered Laughton, eagerly; "it was a bad wound, and it left an ugly scar. Was this scar on—on the body?"

"I hadn't noticed it; in fact, I thought it wasn't there, but to make sure I telegraphed the coroner, and here's his reply."

He held out a yellow slip of paper, which Laughton seized and read greedily. It said that there were no scars on the left arm of the body except near the wrist.

"Fred's wound was in the upper arm near the shoulder," Laughton declared when he had read the telegram. "Then he is not dead! Thank God for that!"

"You are altogether in too much of a hurry, Uncle Larry," suggested the reporter. "This doesn't prove that Fred isn't dead, not at all. But it does make it very improbable that this is his body. We must look elsewhere now. In the meantime, we wanted to make sure about this corpse; and we are trying to find out who the man was, who was found dead wearing Fred's clothes."

" Have you found out ? "

" Bob White asked me to go up and see Inspector Barnes; and I did, and I showed him the paragraph which was in the man's pocketbook. There were three or four First Ward politicians mentioned in that paragraph, regular heelers. Now that was a clue."

" How so?" asked Laurence.

" It was a little bit of a clue, but it was big enough to pull up a string by. If this man cut out a paragraph about a lot of First Ward heelers, he probably knew them, and perhaps they know him. And when a man who has on a second-hand suit of clothes, and who has twenty dollars in his pocket, in a brand-new pocket-book too, and who was alive on the morning of election day, is found floating in the bay a week after election, it is a fair inference that when he was alive he was a cheap politician, a loafer, a worker, as they call them now, who had been 'set up' or 'staked' by his boss on election morning, who bought a swell second-hand suit of clothes, and who got into an election-day row,

at the end of which he found himself in the
river. That's what Inspector Barnes thinks, and
before the week is out we hope to know all about
the man who owns the remains now at Bay
Ridge."

"But you are sure now that it is not Fred's
body?" Laughton asked, anxiously.

"Oh, yes, I'm sure enough, but I shall be
surer yet when I know whose body it is. It
will be a pure joy to me to restore those remains
to the rightful owner—and it will give the
Gotham Gazette a beat on all the other papers."

Laughton lighted a little cigar and sat back in
his chair. "If you find out who this man is,
it will help us to find out what has become of
Fred."

"I don't see why?"

"Because as this man had on Fred's clothes
probably, and certainly his watch, perhaps he had
a hand in robbing Fred."

"That's so," said Brackett; "and now you
put it that way, I don't see how the man came to
have both Fred's clothes and his watch. He
could have bought the clothes second-hand, but
where did he get the watch?"

"True," answered Laughton; "it is an extraordinary coincidence that since Fred has been
robbed, one man should have both his clothes
and his watch,—unless he was one of the rob-
bers."

"I don't believe he was. Of course, he may have had a hand in it—some of those ward-politicians are game for anything; but I doubt it."

"When do you expect any news?"

"Inspector Barnes has his men at work now," replied Brackett, taking his hat to go, "and we may strike the trail at any minute."

Uncle Larry rose and again offered a cigar to his visitor, whom he accompanied to the door. "You will let me know as soon as you hear anything?" he asked.

"I'll keep you posted right up to date, and if anything has happened to Fred, we will make it hot for the other man—you hear me!" Harry Brackett answered as he went down the steps.

The next day the *Gotham Gazette* alone, of all the New York newspapers, contained the full details of the discovery of Frederick Olyphant's watch on the body of an unknown man found floating in the bay.

Two days later the *Gotham Gazette* was able to show that the body in the hands of Coroner Stennett, at Bay Ridge, was that of one Micky Oliver, a First Ward loafer, who had served one term in State prison for 'repeating.' The body was positively identified, from the scar on the wrist, by his brother, the keeper of a low sailor's boarding-house. At the inquest it was brought out that Oliver, after having been very hard up for months, suddenly appeared on the Saturday before election, with a fine suit of clothes, a new hat, a gold watch and chain, and a well-filled pocket-book. The manner of his death remained without explanation.

CHAPTER XII.

A MESSAGE FROM THE MISSING.

IT will be remembered by those who are familiar with the chronicles of New York society that the winter of 1884–85 was one of the most brilliant on record, and that the season began unusually early. As a general rule, the great balls of the year are given in the ten or twelve weeks between the first of December and Ash Wednesday. But this year the Van Siclen ball, which proved to be altogether the grandest affair of the winter, took place on the fourteenth of November. It was given to celebrate the nuptials, so the 'society reporters' informed the world, of Miss Miranda Hitchcock, the only daughter of the great lawyer, Abner Hitchcock, the senior partner of the firm of Hitchcock & Van Renssellaer, with Mr. Edward Van Siclen, the only son and heir of old Schermerhorn Van Siclen, who was at once the leading representative of one of the oldest families of the Knicker-bocker aristocracy, and one of the chief operators in Wall Street. In the famous corner in Transcontinental Telegraph, old man Van Siclen had squeezed Sam Sargent to the tune of nearly two millions; and although Sargent had since made another million or so 'on the Street,' he had not wrenched it from Van Siclen, who had added the two millions of spoils to the snug little sum he had already accumulated. It was the contemplation of this snug little sum thus neatly rounded out, which suggested to old man Van Siclen that he ought to do something for society, and he seized at the occasion of his son's wedding to give a ball. Of course, it would have been more in accordance with the usages of society, if the ball had been given by the bride's parents, but hypercriticism like this did not debar any one from accepting Mrs. Van Siclen's invitation. Even during the excitement of the election, rumors were flying about as to the wonders which the Van Siclen ball was to disclose, and, as soon as the election was once settled, society gave itself up to the ball. It was understood that a temporary ball-room was to be built over the garden in the rear of the Van Siclen house; and it was informally asserted that the supper would be served as soon as the first guest arrived, and that it would continue to be served on demand until the last guest departed. Mrs. Van Siclen had been heard to say that she intended that it should be as easy to get terrapin or canvas-back at five o'clock in the morning as it was at midnight.

The invitations had been sent out nearly six weeks in advance, and before most of those invited had returned to town. Laurence Laughton had found his awaiting him when he got back from Europe, the first week in October. He had accepted at once, as he took a curious delight in the passing show; but as the time drew nigh and there was no news of Frederick Olyphant, he gave up all idea of going. In the fortnight since Olyphant's disappearance, in the week since he had learned of Winifred's engagement to Fred, Laurence had tasted the bitterness of life, and he had learned to look on existence with a seriousness hitherto foreign to his light-hearted nature. He had never held with Gay, that " Life is a jest and all things show it," and he had done his work in the world nobly and earnestly, cheerfully, yet seriously. But to him the work had been easy in the main, and usually he went at it with a light heart. Now, alas, he saw the world as through a gray curtain, and he felt as though the light had gone out of his life. In sheer joyousness of existence he had never before thought that the question, " Is life worth living? " was worth discussion. A great change had come over him, moral rather than physical, though the lines on his face were tense and set as they never had been before. His friends told him that he was not looking well, and advised him to take a holiday. He shook his head

gently and answered that he had work to do. He
was as thoughtful of others as ever, and as
considerate and kind-hearted. Those who relied
on him for advice found him as prompt and as
apt as he was wont to be.

He had not seen Winifred since the Duchess's
dinner to Dear Jones and his bride, and he
wondered why she had looked at him appeal-
ingly, as though she had something to communicate if she only might venture. He did not
dare to conjecture how the newspaper articles,
now appearing every morning and every evening,
might affect her. He loved her, but he had to
confess to himself that he knew little of her
character or of its strength. That she was a
woman with unusual force of will, and an
abnormal power of self-restraint, he knew; and
he believed that he had seen enough of her to
guess that the haughty coldness which struck
strangers as her chief characteristic was but the
thin shell masking a tender, loving, passionate
nature. It was the outward sign of the reserve of a
proud and sensitive girl, conscious of strong feelings, and knowing herself capable of a depth of passion of which she chose not to be suspected. He
knew all the circumstances of the strange story of
her birth, and he knew how these circumstances,
and the cloud of gossip which always encompassed
her about on account of these circumstances, must
have fretted her sensitive soul from her youth up.

About ten o'clock on the night of the great Van Siclen ball, Laurence Laughton was silently pacing the ground floor of his house, now resolutely thinking out the problem of Olyphant's disappearance from those rooms exactly a fortnight before, and now letting his thoughts run away to Winifred Marshall, her beauty, his hopeless love for her, the sad history of her childhood, and the appeal to him which he fancied he had read in her eyes when last they met. So absorbed was he in his thoughts, both bitter and sweet, that he did not hear the ring of his door-bell, nor the passing of the faithful Bridget to answer it. It was not until the parlor-door opened, and a lady entered, that he was aroused from his meditation.

As he paused in his walk to take note of this unexpected interruption, the lady threw back her hood. It was Pussy Palmer, dressed for the ball, and with her hair glittering with diamonds.

"Miss Palmer!" Laughton cried, in astonishment.

"And Miss Palmer is not alone," replied the vivacious Pussy, as another lady appeared in the doorway by her side. "Guess who this is?"

"Winifred!" cried Laughton, as she threw off the lace veil which had covered her head; "Miss Marshall, I mean."

"You didn't expect us, *did* you, Uncle Larry?" asked Miss Pussy.

Laurence did not answer her; he was gazing at Winifred. To his mind, he had never seen her look more radiantly beautiful. The full ball-dress revealed to the best advantage her superb figure, well developed despite its girlish grace. The face was weary and sad, and there was a burning spot on each cheek which told of excitement. As she entered the room, she gave him a frank and appealing look from her honest and trustful eyes: it was the same look he had seen in them a week before.

"It's a surprise party Winnie and I have got up for you," continued Pussy, "and you are very rude not to say you are delighted to see us."

"But I am delighted," answered Laughton, recovering himself, "and I hasten to say so."

Winifred stood still near the door, and from the burning red spot of her cheeks, a blush spread slowly over her face and neck.

"Have you forgotten that it is leap-year?" the lively Miss Palmer went on, with a certain bewitching friskiness of manner suggesting the amusing ways of a little kitten, and thus giving point to her nickname. "Have you forgotten that there is only one more month? We old maids must seize time on the fly, or we shall lose our last chance. Can't you *guess* what we are here for? It's only to ask you to marry one of us; take your choice; if you don't see what you want, ask for it, and *please* report any incivility to the proprietor!"

" Oh, Pussy! " was Winifred's reproachful interruption.

" I'm all right, Winnie; I'm breaking the ice,
that's all," explained Miss Palmer in self-defence.
" It wouldn't do to tell Uncle Larry, all at once,
that we have come on important business."

" You are welcome here always, whatever may
bring you," said Laurence ; "now sit down and
make yourselves at home."

" If you don't mind, Uncle Larry, I'll let my
maid help me off with my things; she's in the
hall;" and Pussy Palmer stepped to the door,
and cried, " *Venez donc, Titine!* "

As a neat-looking French maid entered the
room and said *"Bon soir, M'sieu,"* Pussy explained
that "Ernestine doesn't speak a word of English,
so you can talk right out in meeting just as if
she was a graven image."

Ernestine aided the two girls in removing
their cloaks, which she placed on the piano.

" Now, Uncle Larry, let's be serious," began
Pussy, glancing about the room with a short-
sighted, half closing of the eye-lids, an involuntary
trick of hers, which Mr. Hobson-Cholmondeley
had declared to be " very fetching."

"Am I not serious ?" said Laurence, in a tone of
voice which made Winifred gaze at him earnestly
and wonderingly.

" We have come here for a talk, a consultation
with you—at least, Winnie has ; and I came to play

13

propriety," Miss Palmer continued, with the hearty frankness which was one of her characteristics.

Laughton turned toward Winifred, whose blush came back again, though she met his eyes calmly and steadily.

" Miss Marshall knows that she may command me," said Laughton, inwardly chafing against the cold formality of the phrase.

" Then you give me a book ; anything will do. I never read, you know, so everything is bound to be fresh to me; and I'll take a seat in the library with Titine here, and Winnie can have her talk out with you."

Laughton crossed to the case where he kept his French books, and he took down two. He gave 'l'Abbé Constantin' to Miss Palmer, and he handed to Ernestine one of the adventurous tales of M. Fortuné du Boisgobey. He rolled a comfortable arm-chair before the hickory fire in the library, and he saw Miss Pussy curl herself up in it as snugly as she could without damaging her gorgeous apparel.

Then he went back into the parlor, where Winifred still stood motionless, with her arm resting lightly on the piano. She started forward impulsively, with outstretched hand.

" Mr. Laughton," she said; "I mean, Uncle Larry, for it is only by thinking that you have been kinder than a relative that I am encouraged to come to you. I felt that I must come; I could not help it. I know you are surprised to see me here, and in this dress. You need not deny it; your eyes betrayed you."

Laurence had been about to protest, but he changed his mind. He recognized her as a woman to whom a man might tell the truth. He drew up a chair for her. When she was seated, he sat down in front of her.

" I wanted to see you," she said; " I have wanted for a week, but I had no chance till now. I told Pussy, and it was she who suggested our coming here to night on our way to the ball. Yes; you may well look surprised. I know all you can say, and I feel it myself more than you can say it. The man I love, the man I am going to marry, is missing, and people think he may be dead—and here am I dressed for a ball. And I shall go to the ball, and dance, and try to be merry, while my heart aches. I shall have as good a time as I can; if I did not, I think I should lie down and *die*. I *must* forget for a little while. If I do nothing but think, think, think, all the time, I shall go mad. That's why I am on my way to the ball, and that's why I mean to be as gay as I can."

She paused for a moment, and dried the tears which sprang to her eyes.

" Of course, I should not do this," she continued, " if people knew that I was engaged to Fred, for it would not be paying him the respect he deserves; but nobody knows it, and I am free to do as I please, and to govern my life as I like. It's a poor privilege, but I may as well take advantage of it." She twisted up the handkerchief which she had moistened with her tears. "That is why I am going to the ball," she said, resolutely. "Now, I will tell you why I am here." She looked about the parlor with a yearning curiosity, and the tears came afresh. "I wanted to see the room where he was last; and I wanted you to tell me all about it, all about his sudden disappearance."

Laurence had been watching her, with infinite pity in his eyes. "I shall be glad to tell you anything and everything I can," he said, "but do you think that it is best to dwell on—"

She raised her head and sat upright, as she interrupted him: "If I can bear to read it in a cruel newspaper, cannot I hear it from you? Do not deny me this;" and the resolute ring in her voice softened into pleading tones. "Tell me the whole story, *everything*. I want to hear it all. Begin at the beginning and go on to the very end."

Thus adjured, Laurence did as she bade him. He began at the beginning, and told the whole story. She listened with glistening eyes, glancing about the room as he set forth the strange sequence of events.

When he had come to the end of the tale, she

sat silent for a few moments. At last, she drew a long breath and raised her head again. "It is no use," she sighed. "I cannot understand it. I do not see how he went out, or why. But I know he is not dead!"

"You know it?" asked Laurence.

"I feel it, I am sure of it. Why, Uncle Larry, he is all I have in the world, and if I lose him, what have I left?"

Involuntarily, Laurence held out his hand to her. She took it without hesitation, and returned the gentle pressure.

"I know I have you, Uncle Larry, and Pussy, and I have other friends, too, who are kind to me, in their way, but I *loved* him!"

Laurence bore this without wincing; he stiffened a little, but he made no other sign.

"I have found life lonely enough, at best, and desolate enough," Winifred continued, "but if he were dead—" Here the tears filled her eyes again, and her rising sobs choked her.

"But he is not dead. I shall see him again. I do not know why he went or where he is, but I shall see him again—that I know, as I know anything. I cannot think what has become of him, but he is not dead."

Laurence caught the contagion of her faith, and his doubt gave way to hope.

"Then you do not think he went away from here of his own accord?" he asked.

" Of course not," she replied. " Why should he ? I was here."

Laurence felt the force of this confident expression of trusting affection.

" And he has not committed suicide, as some people foolishly suggest ; of course, they do not know him as I know him. Why should he commit suicide ? He must have been certain of my love for him. You do not think he could have doubted that, Uncle Larry, for all I teased him so, and treated him so shamefully ? "

Fortunately for Laurence, he saw that he was not expected to reply. To express her pent-up feelings was a great relief to Winifred, but she looked for no commonplace consolation.

" I did behave badly to him ; how I wish he were here that I could beg his pardon." She stretched out the damp handkerchief slowly, and then suddenly crushed it into a ball as she looked up again and said, "We had quarrelled; that is what has made me feel so badly. It was all my fault, of course; he was always kind and generous; and I shall never forgive myself, never." For the first time Winifred Marshall broke down completely; she laid her head back wearily and sobbed. She had a strong will, and she used it. She set her teeth and stopped the sobs. Then she sat erect, and said, "I must not give way like this. If I give way now, I am lost. I must keep up somehow, and I will." She drew a long breath, and looked Laughton straight in the eye.

" Before we quarrelled he had begged a ring of mine, and I let him wear it, because he had lost his own. Mine was an opal, and I suppose it was that which has brought this bad luck ; he was always superstitious about stones, and I see now that he was right. I thought he would come in the morning to give me my ring back again, but he never came. I waited for him all the morning, but he did not come. Nothing came but a letter."

" A letter ? " said Laurence, in surprise.

" Yes, he wrote me from here," she answered.

" I remember now," rejoined Laurence, recalling the note Olyphant had asked the faithful Bridget to post for him.

" As he did not come to me, I thought I would go to him. It was Saturday afternoon, and his studio was always open to visitors. Pussy went with me, but he was not there. We went up to the studio, and I found the ring he had lost."

" So it was you ? " said Laughton.

" Did you hear of us ? " she replied. " I found the ring in his studio ; it is a cat's-eye, and I have it now ; and he has mine. The cat's-eye is lucky, you know, and he lost his ; and the opal is un-lucky and he is wearing mine. It is no wonder we are all in doubt and trouble."

" You said you had a letter ? " Laurence inquired.

"Yes," she answered, with a return of the blush.

Laurence saw the color cover her face, and would have been glad to have said no more, but he had no right to neglect any possible source of information as to Olyphant's fate. "Did it contain any suggestion as to his future movements?" he asked, gently, taking his eyes from hers.

"No," she answered, firmly; "but you shall see it; perhaps it is best." She put her hand into her dress, where the letter lay concealed, next to her heart. "Here it is," she said, and she kissed it. "I will read it to you."

"It may not be necessary,—if you think—"

"I will read it," she said, with gentle firmness; "it is better that I should, and it comforts me to hear him say that he loves me."

She unfolded the letter and began to read it:—

"My darling Winifred:

"I am here at Uncle Larry's, and the boys are having a good time in the dining-room; I have left them for a moment to write to you. I could not let the night go by without telling you that I love you, and that I cannot live without you. My head is in a whirl of agony at the thought of losing you. I do not remember what we said to one another this afternoon—and why should we recall hard words spoken in anger? I do not remember why we quarrelled, but I confess now that it was my fault; I know it could not have been yours, Winifred. I am infirm of temper at times, as you have seen, and I may try your patience sorely,—but you will make the best of me, won't you, my darling? I am altogether unworthy of you—I know it only too well—but I love you, I love you, I love you! Forgive me, then, because of my love. Forgive me, my darling, and let me come to you to receive my pardon, for the last time, for there must never again be any disagreement between us. If we quarrelled again, perhaps you could not forgive me again ; and if I lost you, I should lose all there is in the world worth living for and working for. Life is of no use to me, without you.

"Good-night, my darling. I shall feel better now that I have begged you to forgive me. Forgive and forget is a poor motto for me just now, for I want you to forgive me, but if you were to forget me, I should die.

"Good night, once more, my Winifred.

"Your Fred."

Winifred read this through to the end without again breaking down, although her voice trembled as she lingered over the tender words.

"There," she said to Laurence, "you see he is not dead. He cannot be dead; I love him so, oh, Uncle Larry, I love him so! I think of him day and night,—even in my prayers to God, my

thoughts wander to him.   It would be so hard to
lose him—I could never love any one else.   Oh,
Uncle Larry, can't you do something to comfort
me?   I know he is not dead, but I am so miserable while he is away!"

And again the tears flooded her eyes, and she
bent her head forward, weeping over the hand
which Laurence had extended in sympathy.

"You were his best friend, and so I came to
you.   But I know there is nothing to be done.
I must be brave and wait; he will come back to
me.   Do not mind my crying—there, you see I
have stopped; I can cry and nobody will guess
it ten minutes after."

The clock in the library struck eleven.

"Come, girls," said Pussy Palmer, closing her
book, and rising; "time's up."

"I know it," answered Winifred; "I will be
ready in a minute.   I wonder if girls in the
country who read about girls in the city going
to balls ever think that they may take sad hearts
with them.   But if going to balls will help me
keep up my courage, I shall go; and I shall do
my best to enjoy myself, as I know Fred would
want me to.   I must swim on the topmost wave
of society and gaiety; if I go under for a second
I shall drown.   And I must not drown or die; I
must be ready for him.   He will come back to
me, I know it.   All I have to do is to keep up
till he comes to me."

These last few words had been said with feverish volubility, and the red spot in her cheek
burned fiercer than ever. She threw on her
cloak, hastily fastening it at the throat, and she
took up the bunch of yellow roses she had held
in her hand as she came in.

" I have to thank you, Uncle Larry, for listening to me patiently. I know I have troubled
you, but it relieves me so to talk to a kind friend
on whose strength I feel I can lean."

Laurence answered that she might always
rely on him. Ernestine gathered up their
belongings, and there was a rustle of trains, and
then they were gone. He put them into the
carriage ; and as he came up his steps he felt the
first drops of the storm which had been threat-
ening all the afternoon. Before he could get on
his overcoat, the rain was falling in torrents ; he
buttoned the coat about him and walked forth
into the storm. He went up Fifth Avenue, passing the brilliantly-lighted mansion of Schermerhorn Van Siclen, and thrusting himself through
the crowd of curious spectators who braved the
rain to see the arriving guests as they tripped
under the awning from their carriages to the
door. Then he went on up to Central Park,
and he walked around the Park before he
turned homeward. The first faint indications of
the dawn were visible in the East as Laurence
Laughton came back to his own house.

CHAPTER XIII.

NO NEWS.

FOR days, for weeks after the unexpected visit of Winifred Marshall and Pussy Palmer to Laurence Laughton, there was no news. There was absolutely no change in the situation; and the anxious inquirers, despite all their efforts, were no nearer to a solution of the mystery of Olyphant's disappearance. All that money could do, was done; and, at Laughton's expense, the leading detectives of New York had put their wits to work to find a clue which might lead them into the heart of the labyrinth. It was all in vain. Thanksgiving came and went, leaving in the hearts of Olyphant's friends, and of the woman who loved him, no new cause for giving thanks. Day followed day, and week followed week, and they remained in the same mist of uncertainty and doubt.

One day in December, Laurence Laughton received a note from Robert White, asking him to go with him that afternoon to the Police Headquarters in Mulberry Street, to see Inspector Barnes, who had requested them to call, as he had something to communicate. Laughton and White presented themselves in the office of the inspector at the hour he had named. He received them with the same courtesy he had displayed on their previous visit.

" It is a very little bit of news I have for you, gentlemen," he said, when they were seated.

" Every little helps," suggested White.

" No man despises trifles less than I," replied the inspector. " If my experience has taught me nothing, it has at least taught me this—many a mickle makes a muckle, as the Scotch say."

" What is your mickle ? " asked Laughton.

" Only this," answered the inspector: " On the night that Mr. Olyphant was missing, a Greek named Constantine Vollonides left New York on the midnight train for Chicago. This Greek bore a grudge against your friend, and you think it possible that he had a hand in the disappearance?"

" I am convinced of it," Laughton declared.

" Very well," continued Inspector Barnes; " in that case we shall have accomplished something, if we can lay hands on the Greek."

" Have you got him ? " interrupted Laughton, eagerly.

" No," answered the officer, " but we have news of him. I have been trying for now nearly a month, in fact, ever since you first came to me, to trace this Vollonides. Only last night I received the first definite information of a kind that I could rely on. The Greek bought a ticket for Chicago, and he left New York on the midnight train for Chicago; that was all we knew. I could not find out whether he ever arrived in Chicago or not. Now as I say, I have trustworthy information that he left the train probably at Buffalo, though he may possibly have alighted at Niagara Falls."

"What is to be done now?" Laughton asked.

"We must first ascertain whether he is still in Buffalo or Niagara, or whether he simply got off the train there to throw us off the track. I have written to the chief of police at both places, asking them to look the man up, and to let me know as soon as they find any trace of him."

"Do you think he is there now?" White inquired.

The inspector thought for a moment, and then answered, "No, I do not. I am of the impression that his alighting there was only a blind. He may have doubled on his tracks, and returned here, or he may have gone to Chicago by one of the other lines of railroad. It would be well to have Chicago searched as well as Buffalo."

"I will attend to that," said Laughton.

"And, of course," continued the inspector, "we have no right to assume that Chicago was really his objective point. He may have gone there, or he may not."

" It can do no harm to have him looked for there as well as in Buffalo," Laughton declared.

" Certainly not," said the inspector.

" And he may even have gone to San Francisco," added Laughton. " I know that he had a brother somewhere in Southern California."

There was a slight pause in the conversation, and then Inspector Barnes asked : "Have either of you gentlemen ever seen this Greek ? "

" I have," Laughton answered.

" Would you recognize anything belonging to him ? " the officer inquired.

" I might," said Laughton, doubtfully.

" A ring, for instance ? "

" I do not recall any peculiar ring of his," Laughton replied; " but perhaps I should if I saw it."

" When he quit the cars at Niagara or Buffalo he left a ring behind him.   It was found by one of the men who clean up the cars—that's why I have been so long in getting any news; the man hoped to keep the ring for himself. But he was seen to pick it up by another man, who remembered that it had been worn by a passenger on the midnight train, very like the Greek as you have described him to me. Besides, Vollonides arrived here on the *City of Constantinople*, did he not ? "

" Yes," answered Laughton, " only a few hours before Fred disappeared."

" I find that it is the custom of the line to give out charts of the course of the ship, on the back of which is printed a list of the passengers. A chart of this sort, with a list of the passengers on the *City of Constantinople*, was found with the ring. It was rolled up, and the ring had been put on it, much as a napkin ring is put on a napkin."

" Have you the ring ? " asked White.

" Here it is," answered the inspector, taking it from his desk.

Laughton held out his hand for it, and as soon as Inspector Barnes laid the ring on his palm, he walked to the window that he might get a good look at it. Even by the fading light of a December afternoon, he knew the ring at once.

" Do you recognize it ? " asked the inspector.

" I do," answered Laughton.

" Then it belonged to the Greek ? " said White.

" No," replied Laughton, slowly; " it belongs to the young lady Olyphant was engaged to. She lent it to him the last time she saw him. I noticed it on his hand only a few minutes before he disappeared."

" It is an opal," White noted.

" I think you have here another link in the chain which connects the Greek with Mr. Olyphant's disappearance," the inspector remarked.

"Your friend wore this ring at your house on the night he was missing, and the next day it is found on the seat of the railroad car, where Vollonides had been sitting."

"It is scarcely possible to explain this on any other theory than that Vollonides took the ring from Olyphant, after Olyphant left Mr. Laughton's house," White asserted.

"That is the way I look at it," the inspector agreed.

"Then the first thing we have to do is to find the Greek," declared White.

"And when we get him," added Laughton, with a fierceness foreign to his gentle manner, "we'll wring the truth out of him, willy-willy."

"It's like looking for a needle in a haystack to try and find one man out of the fifty millions in these United States. But we shall do it sooner or later," White added.

"You may count on my aid," said Inspector Barnes.

But even with the aid of Inspector Barnes they did not find Constantine Vollonides; and they did not find Frederick Olyphant. Both men had vanished and made no sign. They had disappeared as completely as though the earth had opened and swallowed them up. Buffalo was scoured by the detectives, and Niagara, but with no result. Chicago was searched as it had never

14

been searched before, but no trace of the Greek was found. Laurence Laughton had offered a reward large enough to stimulate the interest of every detective in the United States, but their diligence and industry and vigilance were not profitable.

The dull days followed one another more slowly than ever, and they brought no change. There was always the same inexplicable mystery. Christmas came, but Providence did not vouchsafe to Winifred Marshall the one Christmas gift which she longed for with all the passionate earnestness of her nature. New Year's day followed Christmas, and the new year did not open any more brightly for her than the old year had closed.

In January the newspapers exposed a gigantic scheme of blackmailing which had been planned with extraordinary astuteness, and a singularly acute knowledge of the weak side of human nature. Certain developments in the case led Robert White to believe that the scheme had been in preparation for a long while, and that its originators might have been accomplices in the capture of Frederick Olyphant. Incredible as it might appear, the journalist convinced himself that the outlaws had considered the possibility of adding to blackmail the profits of holding prisoners to ransom ; in other words, they were pre-

pared to transplant to the United States in the nineteenth century the methods and practices of the
brigands of Greece. But it did not take White
very long to discover that he was on a false scent,
and that the reckless plotters whose elaborate
devices for trading on the weaknesses of their
fellow-men had filled the newspapers for days,
could not have shared in the abduction or the
murder of Frederick Olyphant. By personal
investigation he assured himself that they had
no knowledge of Constantine Vollonides, and that
they could tell him nothing about Olyphant's fate.

The winter drew slowly to a close, but the
brightening skies brought no good news to fulfill
the hopes by which Winifred Marshall was
buoyed up. Just before Lent began a party of
her friends set out for New Orleans, to see the
Mardi Gras processions. Mr. and Mrs. Delancey
Jones, and Mr. and Mrs. Charles Sutton, headed
the party, and they asked Winifred and Pussy
Palmer to join them. Winifred refused at once.
She told Mrs. Jones that she did not know when
Fred would return, but it was her duty to remain
in New York that he might find her at once when
he sought her. Pussy Palmer was very anxious
to go; she said she thought it would be " dead
loads of fun"; she tried to persuade Winifred
to change her mind: but when she found that
her friend was fixed in the determination to

remain in New York, she magnanimously remained also, knowing that Winifred relied on her
companionship.

As it happened, Miss Pussy Palmer had her
reward in this world.   Schermerhorn Van Siclen
and his family were hugely delighted with the
success of their great ball, and they were moved
to astonish society again. Young Mrs. Van Siclen,
the bride, formerly Miss Miranda Hitchcock, was
a young lady of fertile invention, and she suggested a fish-dinner for the first week in Lent.
Mr. Van Siclen's father had been a Long Island
fisherman, a fact to which he sometimes referred,
much to his wife's disgust ; and he accepted the
fish-dinner as highly appropriate.   He determined also that as the Van Siclen ball had been
the great ball of the season, so the Van Siclen
fish-dinner should deserve and demand record
in the annals of the highest gastronomy.   The
ingenuity of the Van Siclens and of their professional advisers was tasked to the utmost to
furnish variety.   In the centre of the table was a
huge block of ice, frozen in which, as though
swimming, was a little school of sea-robins, whose
variegated colors were illumined by half a
dozen tiny electric lamps, also frozen into the
block of ice. Other of these little lamps were concealed here and there amid the flowers on the table.
The oysters on the half shell reposed on thin
disks of ice.   There was a clam-soup and

there was a *bisque* of crabs which surpassed description. There was terrapin which pleased even the old bachelors. There was pompano, and there was every other fish which could be procured for love of money. The ice-creams simulated the humble - red-herring; and the finger bowls had tiny gold-fish swimming about in them. These were joys which Pussy Palmer would have lost had she gone to New Orleans for Mardi Gras; and as she was amused by the successive courses with their surprises, she was very glad that she had remained in New York.

"I tell you what," she said to Mr. Hobson-Cholmondeley, who had taken her into dinner, "it *pays* to be self-sacrificing. Virtue is its own reward, and honesty is the best policy."

"*C'est vrai.*" Mr. Hobson-Cholmondeley replied. "Who ever would have thought you had so many kinds of fish here? I've seen more fish here to-day than I ever saw in London, you know; and yet we Britishers live on an island, and we ought to have no end of fish."

The gossip must be recorded here which asserts that Mr. Hobson-Cholmondeley had been very attentive to Miss Pussy Palmer all winter. Charley Sutton had seen them together, and he had remarked that it looked as though "Hob-Chum was beginning to take notice."

Mrs. Martin, who had long before this discov-

ered the good qualities concealed beneath the
young girl's extravagance of speech, had
resolved that she should marry the little Englishman; and it was generally believed that the
Duchess of Washington Square was a special
partner with heaven in the business of match-
making—to use a phrase of Dear Jones's. Mr.
Hobson-Cholmondeley had been heard to declare that he had had enough of globe-trotting,
and that he meant to get a wife and settle down.
" Better get one with money," suggested Charley
Sutton, " and then you can settle up." Mr.
Hobson-Cholmondeley flushed scarlet : " I don't
owe you anything, do I ? " he asked, uncomfort-
ably ; that he was sometimes impervious to a
joke was the chief defect of his character. " You
don't owe me anything but respect," answered
Charley Sutton ; " and I'll lend you a piece of
advice. If you want to get married, hang out a
sign, ' Eligible Bachelor For Sale,' and maybe
some pretty girl will run away with you."
" That's not half bad, that idea," Mr. Hobson-
Cholmondeley had said ; " but do you think it
would be good form ? "

Pussy Palmer confessed to herself that she
was very fond of the little Englishman, and she
looked favorably on his timid suit. People said
she flirted with him outrageously, but Mr. Hobson-Cholmondeley had not complained. Any one
who watched them, as they sat side by side at

the Van Siclen fish-dinner, would have ventured a guess that they were interested in each other. Miss Pussy had allowed her rich auburn hair to grow into the most enchanting little curls, and she had arranged it with consummate art to set off her radiant complexion, which was " as clear as a spring morning after a heavy dew " : so Rudolph Vernon had once described it.

" I'm getting old," she said ; " I'm losing all my illusions, and my dolly is stuffed with sawdust."

" *Tiens, tiens*," chirped Mr. Hobson-Cholmondeley, making a mental record of the curious fact that in America young ladies out in society still played with dolls.

"I used to think once," Pussy continued, " that I might have what I wanted the next day, now I don't expect it till next week, and I don't *always* get it even then."

" What ever do you want that you do not have? " asked Mr. Hobson-Cholmondeley.

" Oh, *lots* of things. I wanted to go to New Orleans, but I'm glad I didn't go, now. I wanted to get out of teaching a class in Sunday-school. I want, most of all perhaps, to learn to control my temper ; why, yesterday at lunch, I got so mad with myself, that I should have talked scripture, if there hadn't been ladies present."

" Oh, indeed? " said Mr. Hobson-Cholmondeley, meditatively.

" Of course," she went on, " the one thing I'd give anything to see, is to see Fred Olyphant come back."

" But you never will see that, you know," Mr. Hobson-Cholmondeley declared.

" Why not ? " she asked, fiercely.

" Because he is dead," was the Englishman's answer.

" How do *you* know ? "

" I am sure of it. He walked out of the little door in Mr. Laughton's library, the one covered by a curtain, you know, and he walked right to the Battery and was drowned."

" I don't believe it. I know he's alive ! " cried Pussy, indignantly ; " and I don't see how you can say such things either."

" *Je dis ce que je pense,*" responded Mr. Hobson-Cholmondeley, a little taken aback by this outburst.

" Then you had better think about something else," returned the American girl.

" But they found his body," persisted the Englishman, not knowing when to stop.

" They didn't do anything of the sort—so, here now ! I am not going to let you brow-beat me in *this* way," the young lady declared, with emphasis. "Frederick Olyphant is alive, and he will come back some day."

" I am afraid not," said Mr. Hobson-Cholmondeley, when he had far better have said nothing.

" But I tell you he will ! " she rejoined ; " and I'll make you think so, too."

" You can't do that, Miss Pussy," he said, with a smile; "really, you know, you can't do that."

" Well, if you want to talk to me, I'll make you wish for his return, for I forbid you ever to speak to me again until Frederick Olyphant comes back ! " And she said this defiantly and firmly ; and the Englishman thought he had never seen her looking as lively and as pretty.

" Come, now, Miss Pussy," he began, " it's really too bad you know—"

" That's enough," she said, rising from the table with the other ladies ; "you have heard the sentence of the court. Until Frederick Olyphant comes back I will not listen to you."

Mr. Hobson-Cholmondeley rubbed his hands together gently as he saw Miss Palmer retreat from the dining-room. But despite his utmost effort and his most effective special pleading he was unable to get his fair judge to reverse her decision.

CHAPTER XIV.

GLAD TIDINGS.

THE fish-dinner of the Van Siclens was the chief topic of talk in the town until the time drew nigh for the inauguration of the new President of the United States, who had been elected four days after Olyphant's disappearance. The enterprising newspapers which had spread before their hundred thousand readers the full bill-of-fare of that Lenten repast, with an illustrative diagram of the dinner-table, placing the guests accurately, and giving a picturesque estimate of their fortunes, individual and collective, were adequate to the new occasion, and kindly provided the future President with ready-made Cabinets reconstructed daily. After the inauguration, the new President appointed his own Cabinet, and the newspapers devoted themselves to chronicling the small-talk of the inauguration-ball. The month of March went out like a lamb, exposing its fleece of snow until its last day, and then April came foolishly forward; but the revolving months left those who loved Frederick Olyphant in the

218

same gnawing uncertainty. He had been gone for five months, and nothing definite had been discovered in regard to his disappearance,— nothing, that is to say, more definite or more precise than the facts which have been set down in the preceding pages.

Winifred Marshall's faith in her lover and in his life did not flag or falter; but hope deferred made her heart sick. The good news was a long time coming. She did not doubt, still less did she despair, but a vague dread began to steal over her, and now and again her strength failed her. She was strong of will, and she nerved herself to conquer a weakness which was almost wholly physical. Yet the struggle told upon her, and the strain was as much as she could stand. Pussy Palmer was with her friend every day, but she could not deny that Winifred had begun to droop and to decline. Pussy feared, so she confessed to Uncle Larry, that if relief did not come soon, Winifred would fade away, and that when Fred did return at last, he would not find his bride. Laurence Laughton saw that Winifred looked wearied and worn. She kept a brave heart, and her beauty grew in pathos; but her body was ready to break down. She had always had High Church ideas, and the fasting she imposed on herself in Lent was more than she could bear. He remonstrated with her in vain, until he told her that she had no right to risk her health, since Fred would not be pleased if he came back and found her weak and waning. She felt the force of this argument, and a few days afterward Laurence noted with pleasure that her walk was firmer, and that there was a fresher color in her cheek. She and Pussy took long rides in the Park every morning, regardless of the inclemencies of the climate. When Easter came, Laughton looked across the church, and he thought she seemed encouraged and refreshed, as though she had obtained some spiritual comfort unknown to him. He could not take his eyes off her during the long service, and when he left the church the dull pain at his heart hurt more than ever before.

The Full Score was to have its Spring dinner at Laurence Laughton's on the Friday after Easter, April 10th, more than five months since the previous meeting, at which Frederick Olyphant had made his last appearance.

In Uncle Larry's dining-room there gathered Poor Bob White and the poetic Rudolph Vernon, Charley Sutton and Eliphalet Duncan, Mr. J. Warren Payn, the composer, and Hobson-Cholmondeley, who had not yet succeeded in getting speech again with Miss Pussy Palmer. Harry Brackett, who had arrived late at the previous meeting, and Dear Jones, who had not been there at all, were also among the guests.

Harry Brackett liked Dear Jones, and he was

greatly given to the humorous banter of those he liked.

"I am told," he was heard to say during a break in the conversation, "that Jonesy is an architect now—not that I have ever seen anything he has built."

"That's because I haven't built a jail yet," retorted Dear Jones.

"Speaking of jails," Brackett continued, imperturbably, "reminds me of what I have also been informed, and that is, that Jonesy studied music and wrote songs and such before he took to building Eastlake pig-pens."

"Somebody once said," Rudolph Vernon remarked, "that architecture was frozen music."

"Do you mean to suggest that Jones's opera would have been a 'frost'?" asked Charley Sutton.

Dear Jones came forward in self-defence. "I never wrote an opera," he explained, "though I did once begin an oratorio on the subject of 'Jezebel'; but I did not advance beyond the composition of a Chorus of Barking Dogs."

"It's lucky you didn't go any further," returned Harry Brackett; "barking dogs don't bite—and musical critics do!"

"Are not all critics dogs?" asked Rudolph Vernon, humorously exaggerating a poet's proper contempt for cynicism.

"I will not allow the critics to be abused,"

Jones declared; " did not one of them say only the other day that a Queen Anne cottage of mine reminded him of the Parthenon ?   It was either the Parthenon or St. Peter's, I forget which."

" The praise of a fool is bitter," said the poet, sententiously.

" But who ever believed that the man who praised him could be a fool ? " Dear Jones inquired.   " I don't.   The man who praises me is a person of remarkable discernment, and of the highest intellectual attributes."

" Of course," assented Eliphalet Duncan.

" I have known critics," said Mr. Hobson-Cholmondeley, judicially, " who were *tant soit peu* commonplace persons."

" Well, I should say so," Robert White responded ; " some critics don't know enough to keep over night.   Why, when I wrote a satirical paper for the *Arctic Monthly*, which I called 'An Inquiry into the Alleged Collaboration of Bacon and Shakspere in writing Punch-and-Judy,' a man in an up-country newspaper called me to account gravely for the insubstantiality of my argument—just as if I could provide not only the merry jest but also the sense of humor for its proper enjoyment."

" I remember a man down-east or out-west, I forget which," said Dear Jones, " who complained of the insubstantiality of Fred Olyphant's ' Vision of No-Man's Land. ' "

" Fancy now," Mr. Hobson-Cholmondeley remarked. " It's something curious to think that
poor Olyphant was at work on a picture called
the ' Sharpness of Death,' when he died himself."

" If he really is dead ? " said White, gravely.

" Dear me," asked Mr. Hobson-Cholmondeley ; " do you doubt it ? "

" Most decidedly I doubt it," answered White.

" So do I," added Laughton.

" Really now," the little Englishman rejoined,
" I wish I could. His death was most unfortunate, for he was a good fellow, you know,
jusqu'au bout des ongles. But I haven't any
doubt that he walked out of that door in the
library, and went down to the Battery, and was
drowned."

" But that was not his body we found," said
Harry Brackett.

" And he did not go out of that door in the
library," Laughton declared, " for it was locked."

" Are you quite sure of that, Uncle Larry ?"
asked Robert White.

" Well, I don't know," said Laughton ; " we
found it locked, you remember, and the key was
on my table up stairs."

" But let us apply what the logicians call the
process of exclusion," persisted White. " Fred
was in this house on the night of October 31st;
he was on this floor, in one of these three rooms,
parlor, library, dining-room. Now, he must

have got out by an opening of some sort. The only openings are the chimneys, windows and doors. The chimneys are too small for human egress. The windows could not have been opened without our knowledge ; it is simply impossible that Fred could have gone into either the parlor or the dining-room and opened a window and got out, without being seen by the men in those rooms. Therefore, he must have made his exit by one of the doors. Now, there are three doors and three only—one in the parlor, one in the dining-room here, and the little one behind the curtain in the library. The door in the parlor is easily disposed of—it was closed, and I was leaning against it : therefore I know that Fred did not go out that way."

"And I know he did not go out by the door in this room," interrupted Charley Sutton, "for I was sitting just in front of it, with my feet up on a chair, and nobody could have passed without disturbing me."

"The door was shut tight," added Rudolph Vernon, "for I remember what a rattle it made as I slid it to."

"Therefore," declared White, "as Fred could not have gone up the chimney or out of the window, and as he did not go out of the door here in the dining-room, or out of that in the parlor, he must have gone out of the little door in the library. Q. E. D."

" That's what I said directly I heard he was gone," said Mr. Hobson-Cholmondeley, rubbing his hands together gently.

" But that little door was locked," Laughton replied.

" It was locked when you tried it; yes. But was it locked earlier in the evening?" asked White. " And when had it been unlocked last before that night."

" I have a vague recollection," answered Laurence, " that it had been open two or three days before, during the cleaning of the house. I told the faithful Bridget, I remember, to lock it up again, when the cleaning was over, and to take the key up to my room. And she must have done it, because we found the door locked and we found the key up stairs."

" That is all very well," White returned; " but it is just as easy to say that Fred must have gone through this door, for he could not have got out any other way; and that he did get out somehow we all know, because the watch he wore and the ring he had on, have been found elsewhere. The door had been open, as you confess: now, why not let us ask the faithful Bridget when she locked it?"

" Well, I don't know," said Uncle Larry, " perhaps you might have her up. I don't suppose she will remember, but it won't do any harm to ask her, and I think she likes to come up when

15

there's company." He told one of the waiters
to request the faithful Bridget to step up stairs.

"You conduct the examination-in-chief," said
Charley Sutton to White, "and I'll cross-examine
for the defence."

"Unless you want every cross-question to
bring a crosser answer," Uncle Larry ventured
to remark, "perhaps it would be best to let me
extract the information."

"I object," Charley Sutton began.

"Of course," interposed Eliphalet Duncan ;
but the court overrules the objection, and allows
the exception."

A pleasant old Irish voice was heard on the
stairs leading up from below calling, "Come
here, sir, come here! Bundle o' Rags! Bundle
o' Rags! Oh, the little wretch, there's no holding
him!" and Bundle o' Rags bounded into the
dining-room at full speed, stopping short by
the side of Uncle Larry, where he threw himself back on his haunches and began to beg at
once.

"Sure, there's no holding him, sir, none at
all. Do what I will, he's out of my hands before
I know where I am," said the faithful Bridget, as
she entered the dining-room, and came to the
head of the table. "Good evening, gentlemen,"
she added, as she saw the assembly.

"How are you, Bridget?" was shouted at her
from all parts of the table.

"It's well I am, barring a taste of the rheumatics in my feet."

As Uncle Larry gave Bundle o' Rags the bone for which he had been mutely pleading since his sudden appearance, he noticed that one of the dog's eyes was abnormally free from the shaggy hair which generally begirt it. "What is the matter with his left eye, Bridget?" he asked.

"Sure, I don't rightly know, sir; I think it's that Cleopatrick, sir, the kitten. They're so playful together there's no keeping them apart. I think when she combed his bang the morning, she stuck her finger in his eye. But she's a good kitten, is that Cleopatrick, sir; there's no harm in her."

"Bridget," Laughton began, "do you remember when that little door in the library was open, the one behind the curtain, I mean?"

"Sure I do, sir," she answered, promptly; "we'd been after cleaning the house, and I had the key down and I opened it."

"Do you remember my telling you to lock it up?"

"Indeed I do, sir. And by the same token I forgot it. As you know, sir, it isn't often I forget my duty, but I clean forgot that, so I did."

Robert White looked at Laughton with a smile of triumph, as the host asked, "Well, when did you lock the door, Bridget?"

"It was for two days I forgot it, sir; but 'twas

no wonder, sir. I was flustered with getting the house ready for the dinner. Sure, 'twas then you had all these gentlemen to dinner."

"And that was two days after I had told you to lock the door?" Laughton inquired.

"Sure it was, sir, and 'twas the night of the dinner I locked it. I was going up to bed, and as I passed the hall here, the door was open and then I minded me, I had to lock it, and I turned the key then, and I took it up to your room, sir."

"You say you found the door open as you passed?" asked Laughton.

"Indeed it was, sir, all along of my not having locked it before. 'Twas open half-way across the hall, as though somebody had been through it, though it was shut in the morning, that I'm sure."

"And what time was it when you went to bed that night?"

"'Twas my regular time, ten or the half after," replied the faithful Bridget.

"That will do, Bridget," said Uncle Larry; "thank you. You can take Bundle o' Rags down with you."

But Bundle o' Rags heard this, and he seized his bone in his teeth and he fled into the parlor, where he hid himself under the furthermost corner of a sofa. The faithful Bridget pursued him swiftly, but he resisted her blandishments and refused to come forth.

"You may let him stay up," Laurence called to her. "I'll attend to his case."

"Very well, sir, if you say so," and the faithful Bridget withdrew.

"It is always mean to say, 'I told you so,' but I cannot resist the temptation just this once," said White to Laughton.

"*Dixi!*" remarked Mr. Hobson-Cholmondeley, "*je vous l'ai dit!*"

Mr. Hobson-Cholmondeley was a kindly, good-hearted little fellow, but as Charley Sutton put it, "he is as obstinate as they make 'em; and he has no more tact than a hedgehog."

"I think it is plain enough now how Fred got out of the room," White declared; "he walked out through the little door in the library, leaving it ajar. The curtain concealed this fact from Uncle Larry. Fred took his hat and left the house. Then, while Uncle Larry was looking for him in the parlor and in the dining-room, Bridget came up to go to bed. She saw the library door open, she locked it and she took the key up stairs to Uncle Larry's room."

"I have always said," Mr. Hobson-Cholmondeley declared, "that poor Olyphant walked out through that little door, and that he went down to the Battery and that he is drowned."

"And I say he isn't drowned," Robert White retorted; "I believe he is alive."

"Then where is he?" asked the Englishman.

" I don't know."

" And why doesn't he turn up? " persisted the obstinate little fellow.

" I don't know," White answered. " But I think he is alive, and I think he will surely turn up."

" So do I," Laughton agreed.

" But there's no common-sense in believing in a thing contrary to the facts," Mr. Hobson-Cholmondeley urged.

" Here are the facts," rejoined White, " and here is my interpretation of them: Fred had no reason to go away and hide ; indeed, he had the best of reasons for staying here. Therefore we may assume that his absence or disappearance is not voluntary. He was known to have a bitter enemy who had a hereditary passion for revenge. We know this enemy arrived in New York a few hours before Fred vanished. Therefore we may believe that this enemy was the cause of Fred's disappearance."

" Do you think Vollonides killed Fred? " asked Charley Sutton.

" No, I do not think so now. If he had killed him he would not have left Fred's ring lying about in a car ; he was too sharp for that. Beside, he was a quick-witted Greek, and he was wily enough and cruel enough to know that instant death is not the worst of fates. To live and to suffer and to know that those we love are suffering, is worse than death, many degrees worse. Now, on the boat which brought him here, Vollonides picked up a bit of information about Fred and—"

"And the man who gave him that information has been kicking himself for a fool ever since," interrupted Jones.

"Quite right too," commented Harry Brackett.

"This information," White continued, "may have made him change his mind. No doubt he had come here to kill Fred. Instead of killing him he preferred to secrete him somewhere, to spirit him away, leaving doubt and dismay behind, and causing many times as much misery as a certainty of death."

"But what has he done with him?" asked Jones; "I'm told that the Bastille is now out of repair."

"And the press-gang has lost its power," added Eliphalet Duncan.

"Twenty years ago," Charley Sutton remarked, "we might have thought he had been shanghaied."

"Shang-what?" asked Mr. Hobson-Cholmondeley.

"Shanghaied—that is, drugged and shipped as a sailor on a vessel bound for Shanghai or any other long voyage."

"Dear me," ejaculated Mr. Hobson-Cholmondeley, "that's something dreadful. Do they do it now?"

"I haven't heard of a case for years now," Charley Sutton answered. "But once upon a time New York was a famous port for Shang-haiers. And a poor devil who was shanghaied was wiped out as completely for the time being as though he had been pressed in England or sent to the Bastille in France."

"*C'est curieux*," said Mr. Hobson-Cholmon-deley, meditatively. Then, turning to Robert White, he asked, aggressively, "So you think poor Olyphant has been shanghaied?"

"I don't say that," White replied; "I have no idea what Vollonides has done to him. But I do not believe that the Greek has killed him, since he knew that doubt as to his fate would be more cruel than death."

"I never went in for subtlety," said Mr. Hobson-Cholmondeley, with dogged determina-tion; "and what I said I stick to. I say poor Olyphant went out of that little door in the library, and that he went down to the Battery and was drowned in the Bay."

"And I say that I think he is alive," retorted White.

"There are mysteries," intervened Rudolph Vernon, "that no man has ever solved. We do not know the name of the man who wore the Iron Mask—"

"And nobody knows who struck Billy Patter-son," Charley Sutton remarked, casually.

"And it may be," continued the poet, disregarding the young Californian's interruption, "that the mystery of Fred's disappearance may also remain unsolved and insoluble."

"It would not surprise me if the bell were to ring at any moment, and if Fred walked right in on us now and here," said Laughton, who had been listening silently.

As if in answer to his words, there came a sharp ring at the door-bell. A sudden hush fell upon the little group of Olyphant's friends. There was a minute of anxious expectation, and then the door opened and the faithful Bridget entered with a telegram-envelope in her hand.

"It's a false alarm," said Charley Sutton, with a sigh. "I wish it wasn't," and the conversation sprang up again as Laurence Laughton took the envelope, and, after a hasty apology, tore it open. He read the telegram in silence, and drew a long breath. Then, without a word he passed it to Robert White. The journalist glanced at it and sprang to his feet. He was younger than Laughton and he had less self-control.

"Is there news?" asked Charley Sutton.

"From Fred?" added Duncan, who was quick to read a face.

"Yes," answered White. "He's alive! and he will be here in a week!"

The Full Score arose as one man and gave a ringing cheer.

The telegram was from Frederick Olyphant in San Francisco. This is what it said :—

" All right. Shall leave here for New York on first train. Break the news to her."

CHAPTER - XV.

THE LAST MEETING.

FREDERICK OLYPHANT'S story — the story of his strange disappearance, of his peculiar adventures, of his existence during the five months and more that he was missing, of the awful fate which was prepared for him by the devilish malignity of his enemy, of his escape from the plot laid against him, and of his last meeting with Constantine Vollonides—can best be told in this place and in his own words, as he set it down at the loving request of Winifred Marshall, who wished to have an exact record of the things which befell her lover while he was away from her.

On the evening of the last day of October, 1884,—so his narrative began—I went to a dinner of The Full Score at Laughton's. After dinner we broke up into little groups. Some of the men remained in the dining-room, smoking over their coffee. Others went into the parlor and stood about the piano, while some one played. Uncle Larry and I were alone in the library. I wrote you a letter and I gave it to

Bridget to post. I had been feeling miserable
ever since I parted from you—and it was no
wonder. After I had written the letter, my
spirits revived a little, though I was dull and
jaded. Larry told me that I had been working too hard, and that I ought to rest. I
recall every word of the talk we had—how I
gave vent to the discouragement which had
possessed me, and how he tried to put heart
into me with the manly kindness I have always
found in him. For once I took no comfort in
his counsel. I knew he was right in saying
that I had worked too hard, and that I had
confined myself too closely. A sense of physical oppression seized me again, and I felt that if
I had not air, and cold, fresh air at once, I should
choke. Uncle Larry, with his back to me, was
bending over the fire, building up the hickory
logs ; there were laughing knots of men in both
the parlor and the dining-room. With a hasty
and perhaps inarticulate word of explanation to
Larry, I pushed through the curtain which
hung across the opening in the bookcase and
concealed the little door leading into the hall.
This door was unlocked, and I passed through
it, leaving it open. Seizing my hat from the
stand in the hall, I stepped out upon the stoop
and stood in the outer air with the house-door
ajar behind me.

Almost opposite Larry's house is one of

the iron masts which support the electric lamps, and leaning against this tall post was a man whose figure seemed to be remotely familiar to me, but to whom I paid no attention at the moment. The sharp air of the chill October night revived me. The avenue was quiet and deserted, and the faint echoes of a noisy torchlight procession crossing Union Square were the only sounds that broke the silence. As I turned to go back into the house, I saw that a man was coming up the steps, and I recognized him as the man I had seen standing against the post on the other side of the street. I could not close the door in his face, and I delayed until he stood beside me.

" Do you wish to see Mr. Laughton ? " I said, turning toward him. His slouch hat was pulled down over his face, and he was muffled in a scarf which concealed his features, yet I saw, or I thought I saw, a man whom I had not met for years. I drew back instinctively, and stood on my guard. Suddenly I became conscious of a strong odor, a strange and pungent perfume of overpowering and enervating fragrance. I recalled dimly that I had met this same curious scent once before in the East at a fortune-teller's, at the house of an old hag, accused of dealing in poisons. My suspicions were aroused, but under the influence of the mysterious and penetrating drug, my will was inert and my muscles were lifeless. I fell forward supinely into the arms of the stranger. I was aware that he closed the door of the house gently, and that he then bore me down the steps to the sidewalk, half carrying me and half aiding my automatic movements. At the corner he stopped a carriage, and then I became wholly unconscious. It seemed as though I were in the power of my enemy, and that he was binding me with cords, and that all my struggles were vain. Then I burst my bonds asunder and soared upward toward an ineffable glory, which shone farther and farther aloft in the etherial space beyond the world. But gradually the light faded away and all was dim, dark, and at last black as midnight. Solitude encompassed me about, and a sense of desolate loneliness weighed me down and chilled me. Slowly I awoke, to find myself full of dull aches and nauseating pain. I was alone and in the dark. There was a rhythmical motion of the flooring under me. As my senses came to me, doubtfully at first, but after a while more clearly, I knew that I was on the water. I staggered to my feet, and in a few minutes I had made sure that I was in the hold of a ship. I had been kidnapped—and the boat was bearing me away from you. My strength returned, and my wrath arose.

For a long while there was no answer to my call. I could hear voices, and the creaking of cordage, and now and again the tramp of feet on deck far above my head. As my eyes became used to the darkness, I saw that I was in the lazaretto, the little compartment often found under the captain's cabin of a sailing vessel. Around me were barrels of beef and boxes of provisions and other of the ship's stores. The only mode of egress from this lazaretto was through the hatch into the cabin above. As no attention was paid to my angry outcry, I heaped up a few boxes and, standing upon them, I began to hammer on the deck above me. When I had nearly worn myself out in the vain effort to force some one to release me, there were footsteps overhead, and the hatch was opened. I was almost blinded at first by the sudden flood of light, and my head was dazed with pain. " Let me out ! " I cried, to the man who had lifted the hatch.

" *Che ?* " he said, in Italian, " what have we here ? "

He was a stout, good-looking and good-natured Italian, and I took him to be the steward of the vessel.

" Let me out ! " I cried, in Italian, thrusting myself up into the cabin. " And now where is the captain ? "

He answered that the captain was on deck. I sprang up the companion-way and stood again in the open air. I was on the deck of an Italian bark of about twelve hundred tons. We were heading east-southeast, and there was a stiff breeze from the northwest. We were out of sight of land. The sun was high in the heavens and it was nearly noon : I had been unconscious for at least twelve hours, and perhaps longer.

As I came on deck the captain was standing amidships, getting ready to take an observation. He was a wily and wiry little Genoese, with sharp and piercing eyes and a full black beard. He turned to me as I rushed up the hatchway, and asked,

"Who is this?"

There was an affectation of surprise in his voice, but angry as I was, I noticed that he seemed not a little uneasy, and that he glanced restlessly about. In answer to his question, a burly ruffian with heavy eyebrows and an evil mouth—he was the first mate—said that I was the sailor who had been brought on board dead drunk.

"I am not a sailor," I declared; "and I was not drunk!"

"Oh ho!" cried the mate. "He was not drunk!—and he was so stupid with drink that we had to hoist him aboard, and put him in the lazaretto!"

"I was not drunk," I repeated, "though I may have been drugged."

"That's a likely story," sneered the mate.

"And I am not a sailor!" I continued, vehemently; "I am an American. I demand that you set me ashore at once."

The captain hesitated a moment, and then seemingly made up his mind. "I have nothing to do with all this. You are engaged as a sailor, and you must do your work and—"

"But I am not a sailor, I tell you!" I repeated.

"You must be a sailor, or why are you here?" the captain returned.

"I do not know why I am here," I replied, "nor how I got here. I am an American—a gentleman—not a sailor! I can prove to you what I say!"

"How?" asked the captain, coldly, keeping his piercing eyes on me.

I was about to say that my note-book, my pocket-book, my watch, would all show that I was what I pretended to be, but as I put my hands to my pockets I saw that my clothes had been changed. I had on a suit of coarse sailor's clothes, and the pockets were empty.

"It seems I have been robbed, too!" I shouted, for I had no longer any control over my temper. "My clothes have been taken from me, and my money and my watch—" and here I saw that the ring you had lent me was gone also—"and an opal ring! I want them back at once, and I want to be set ashore."

"I cannot take my ship back just to oblige a sailor," said the captain.

16

"But I am not a sailor!" I replied, "and I will pay you well."

The captain gave me another piercing glance; then he said, "Enough of this! I have lost time enough. You are now at sea, on my ship, and you must do your work. When we get to port you can go, not before."

"To what port are you bound?" I asked, as I began to feel the helplessness of my position.

"San Francisco," answered the burly mate.

"San Francisco?" I repeated, in horror.

"San Francisco is our port," the mate replied, with a harsh laugh; "and it may be six months before you get ashore."

"Six months!" I cried, in agony. "I cannot do it! Put me ashore now, for the love of God!"

"Enough of this," said the captain again, as he raised his instrument to take the sun. "Have this man go forward!"

"Go forward," ordered the mate, striking me on the shoulder. My heart was full of rage and despair. It was a joy to have some one whom I could hit back. I felt like a wild beast as I sprang at the mate and knocked him down. Two of the crew pulled me from him. He rose to his feet unsteadily and seized a belaying-pin. The men released me, and I looked him in the eye. Without a word he felled me to the deck with a blow of the pin. As I lay motionless he was about to strike me again, when a voice, with a strong Maltese accent, said, " Let him alone now. Do not kill him; we shall want him soon enough if this gale keeps on." Then the same voice said " Take him into the forecastle."

When I came to it was late at night, and I was lying in a bunk in the forecastle. The ship was tossing, and there was a hard gale from the north-west. I lay dozing as it struck eight bells and the men off watch came into the forecastle. They were full of rough sympathy. They told me that the mate was a brute, but that it was lucky I had struck him and not the captain, or I should be at the bottom of the sea with a dagger in my heart. They said that the captain was quiet enough generally, but a very devil when roused. He was half owner of the bark, which was called the *Vengeance of God.* There were thirteen men before the mast, including myself:—I thought of the night before, when we had also been thirteen at Uncle Larry's dinner. With the cook, steward, carpenter, two mates and the captain, we were nineteen all told. The men informed me that I had been put in the starboard watch— the captain's watch, as it is called—where I should be under the second mate, who was a good fellow, kindly and not overbearing; but unfortunately careless. It was the second mate who had interposed to save me. The crew soon turned in and left me alone with myself.

The absolute helplessness of my position burst
upon me with overpowering force, and I knew
the futility of resistance. It was worse than useless for me to rage, to storm, to threaten. The
captain did not fear me, and I could not conquer
him by force. My only chance was to bide my
time, to trust to good fortune to come to my
rescue, and in the meanwhile to make the best of
it. I was alone, miles off shore, in a foreign ship,
without a friend. It took little reflection to
prove to me that I was powerless, that my fate
was no longer in my own control, and that I had
best accept the inevitable with a good grace. I
abandoned all hope of rebellion, and determined
to do my duty while I was aboard the boat, ready
to seize the first chance to leave it.

I knew nothing about the ship, or the captain,
or the crew, but I was aware that the cruelty of
a captain may make his ship a floating hell. I
did not dare to guess what was in store for me,
or what ill-fortune the future might bring forth.
I could not tell whether the captain was the accomplice or the hireling of the man who had
wrought this wrong against me. I did not know
whether I could expect mercy from him, but I did
know that I was wholly in his power, and that my
utmost effort would avail nothing. He could do
with me as he pleased; he could keep me in chains;
he could condemn me to solitary confinement;
he could torture me at will. Yet the fear of these

things did not dishearten me, for I felt that I could bear them,—nay, more, that I would prefer them to the mental anguish I was undergoing. The thought that I had parted from you in anger, that I had been torn from you without a word of explanation or a chance of farewell, that I could not bid you take heart and be of good cheer, that I had left you plunged in depths of doubt which must slowly turn to despair—this was almost more than I could bear. The galley slave, chained to the oar; the prisoner for life, confined in the dark cell; the victim of the Inquisition pinioned to the rack—these may each of them suffer the tortures of the damned (and I foresaw that I might soon be made to suffer as they suffered),—but what was the pain inflicted on the body, however acute, and however prolonged, compared with the protracted agony of soul which I saw before me. The ingenuity of a fiend could have found no keener punishment.

In the morning, when it came the turn of my watch to go on deck, I went with them.

" Ah," said the captain, as he saw me. " You have come to your senses, have you ? Now let's have no more of this nonsense ! "

The gale had moderated during the night, and we were sent up aloft to set all sail, for we had been running under very little canvas. I felt that the captain kept his eye on me, and I did

my work as neatly and as quickly as I could.
You know that I am fond of the sea, and that I
have had my share of experience as a sailor-man.
Even the Italian terms were not strange to me,
for I had been all around the Mediterranean in an
Italian boat.

As I came down from the rigging the captain
called me.

" Here; you ! " he cried.

I came to him.

" You said you were not a sailor," he said.
" You lie, it seems.   You *are* a sailor."

I answered that I had told the truth, and that
I was not a sailor, although I had sailed a boat
many a time, and had even studied navigation.
The captain looked at me as I said this, but he
made no reply.   For weeks after this, he did not
speak to me or take any notice of me ; and yet
I was conscious not infrequently that his sharp
eyes were on me.   He spared me the irons, the
imprisonment, the bodily torture, I had half expected.   In the main, he did not treat his crew
badly, and he treated me as he treated the
others.   Although I felt that he gave me more
attention than he bestowed on the rest of the
crew, yet he did not abuse me or offer me any
indignity.   Except for the constant watchfulness
with which he followed me, he showed the same
indifference to me as to the other men before
the mast.   I studied his face as occasion served,

and I thought it was not the face of a bad man : he was high-tempered and he was weak, rather than evil. I was in doubt whether he was the accomplice of the villain who had betrayed me into his hands. From chance words dropped by the second mate, the friendly Maltese, in whose watch I was, I began to believe that perhaps it was not the captain, but the ruffianly first mate who was responsible for my involuntary voyage. I felt that this fellow hated me. I knew I hated him.

We had a stiff breeze behind us all the way down the coast and across the equator. The weather was warm and delightful. We were making good time. I hoped for a storm which would force us to put into port, but as there seemed no chance of that, I rejoiced that we sailed along as fast as we did. I counted every knot that we made, and I checked off the miles we had yet to make. I did my daily work, the dull routine work of a sailor on a sailing vessel when all sails are set and stay set for weeks at a time. The work was not hard, and it did not employ my thoughts. It occupied my hands, but it left my mind free—and there were days when I thought I should go mad. I saw all the doubt and all the misery that my unexpected departure and inexplicable absence would surely cause. I knew that it might be months and months before word from me could reach you—if it ever reached you at all. I knew that I might never leave the ship alive, and that I might never see land again ; and you would not know what had become of me. I could not fail to imagine the agony and the anguish of uncertainty which you would feel. I thought of it day and night. You were never out of my mind. Yet there was no way out of the misery, and there was no use in rebelling : I must bear it with the fortitude I knew you would show, and it was the thought of your example which gave me strength. Many a night, as I stood on the forecastle looking out over the ocean, I saw you as I had seen you last—in the Bower— through the opening in the screen, half hidden by the vines. I saw you with the bunch of yellow roses at your waist, faintly outlined against the descending dusk. It was a beautiful vision and a gracious memory ; and I loved to recur to it. Though it pained me, it comforted me also. Yet when I saw it, I did not dare to wonder how you accounted for my sudden absence : I knew you loved me and I trusted you.

If it had not been for my thoughts the life would have been endurable ; the *Vengeance of God* was a new boat, and the captain knew his business. The crew were good-natured, and I had their rough sympathy. The second mate was kindly, and I had only the first mate to be on my guard against. The sailors were all afraid of him, and they believed he had the evil eye. He never looked at me without hatred in his glance. Fortunately, I was not in his watch. I paid no attention to him, but did my work quietly and steadily.

Off the Rio de la Plata we got into a pomparo, which is the name they give to a local storm, often found there and peculiar to that region. It began with a black cloud in the northwest, like the first warning of a summer squall. It was the captain's watch, and the second mate was on duty in his stead. This second mate was a jolly and careless Maltese, and he did not take the warning the cloud gave. The captain chanced to come on deck, and the instant he saw the storm coming, he knew what was wanted. We had all sails set. First we took in the royals and then the top-gallant sails. Then we went to work on the flying-jib and the gaff-top-sail; at the same time we clewed the top-sail yards down and close-reefed the main-top-sail. By the time we got these in, it was blowing pretty fresh and we had hard work to take in the fore-top-sail; and, after all, it was no use, for although we got it clewed up the wind blew it clean off. The captain held the second mate responsible for this mishap, and he broke him and appointed me. I refused and pleaded hard for the Maltese. It was no use. The captain was determined that the man should not hold the place any longer. I still refused, but I yielded when the Maltese himself begged me to take the place, suggesting that as I was going to leave the ship at the first port, I might then urge his re-appointment. The first mate, the stalwart ruffian who had struck me, did what he could to prevent my promotion. But I accepted the position. I did not know how large a share the captain had had in my abduction, and I guessed that he might have given me the post of mate as a peace-offering.

I had made early inquiries as to the chance of sending a letter, and I had learned that unless we happened to be stopped by a passing ship— which was most unlikely—the first possible opportunity would be off Pernambuco. There the fishermen put off in light catamarans, and they are often met with in the track of vessels bound around the Horn; they are always willing to take letters, accepting the gift of a bottle of liquor or of a piece of beef as pre-payment of postage. On the chance of sending by a passing ship, I had written a long letter to you; but the days went by and no ship hailed us. We were becalmed for a while in the tropics, and it was quite seven weeks after we had left New York before we came within the range of the Pernambuco fishermen. As the possibility of communicating with you shone nearer and nearer, I felt happier. I began to accept my separation, if only I could tell you where I was and how it was I had been taken away. I wrote you a long letter pouring out the love that filled my heart and strengthened me.

But my spirits sank as rapidly as they had risen when we passed off Pernambuco and no fishing-craft had been seen. It might be, after all, that I was not to have the chance of sending my letter. At last, on Christmas Eve, the look-out cried out first that there was a sail in sight— later, that it was a fisherman's catamaran ; and then I knew that I might send you as a Christmas present news of the man who loved you and longed for you and thought of you, and of you only, day and night, as he sailed further and further away from you.

I told the captain I had a letter to send. He gave me a piercing look from his penetrating eyes, and said that I might put it in his bundle, which was in his cabin. I did so, and by the time I was again on deck, the frail little craft, with two fishermen on board, was almost along-side of us. We hailed them and threw them a rope, and they made fast. The captain gave them a piece of beef in exchange for a few fish. Then he asked them if they would take letters to land for us. They agreed willingly, and the captain sent the mate for the bundle. When it came, he bade the steward get a bottle of spirits, and he passed the bottle and the bundle of letters over the side to the fishermen. Then the catamaran was cast loose, and in a few minutes it had dropped behind us out of sight in the night-fall.

I walked my watch that night with a warm heart, thinking of you and calculating that you might get my letter in less than a month, possibly by the middle of January. But this hope and this joy did not abide with me long.

When we got down to the Horn, we had a fair wind from the north, and the captain tried to go through the Straits of Lemaire, between the mainland of South America and Statenland. But we had scarcely got well into the straits before we struck a heavy gale from the south-west. We had to make a harbor, and in tacking ship, as she came up with her head to the wind, we shipped a tremendous sea, which took the first mate off the forecastle. We never saw him again. The captain made me first mate, and at my request re-appointed the former second mate to his old position. Now that the first mate was gone, I was the only man on board, except the captain, who knew how to navigate a ship; but none of the sailors were jealous of me or be-grudged my advancement. I was told to take possession of the first mate's cabin. The first thing I found there, hidden in a corner, was my letter to you! The evil wretch had stolen it as he brought the letters from the captain's cabin to the side of the boat. I was so happy at the hope of writing to you that I had not suspected him. And now his treachery had plunged me from heaven to hell again. It was lucky for the man that he was dead. Repining was useless, I knew, and I resolved to make the best of my ill-fortune. I had at least the consolation that I had accomplished the half of my journey.

Then the wind failed us, and we made slow sailing for a while. But the longest voyage must draw to an end at last. About a week before we could hope to reach San Francisco, we made land, and I caught my first glimpse of the coast of lower California, and my heart beat high, knowing that I should soon set foot on the soil you trod, though I might be separated from you by thousands of miles.

The Maltese was again the second mate; so far from being jealous of my promotion over his head, he was grateful to me for his reappointment. As we came up the Pacific coast, I became aware that he had a trick of lingering near me, and of hesitating, as though he had something he would like to say, but did not know how to broach the subject. When I was once firmly convinced of this, I waited for a favorable occasion, and then I got him to talk. He began on an indifferent subject, but he soon turned the conversation to the dead mate, the ferocious ruffian who had been washed overboard.

" 'Tis a good thing he is dead," said the Maltese. " He had the evil eye."

" 'Twas a sudden death," I suggested, hoping to lead him on, as I began to suspect that he knew something about my abduction.

" 'Tis not for you to speak for him," returned the Maltese. " He was your enemy, and the friend of your enemy."

" The friend of my enemy," I repeated.

" You are not a sailor," he answered. " You did not come on this voyage willingly. You were sold by an enemy. It was the dead man who brought you on board; and he was paid. There was another man in the boat when he brought you. This man gave him money. This man was your enemy, for he—" Then the Maltese hesitated

" Go on," I cried.

" No, I have said enough," he answered.

" Do you know the other man ? " I asked.

" No," he replied; " I had seen him only once before."

" Where ? "

" In front of ' Oliver's.' "

I knew that " Oliver's " was a sailor's boarding-house of the worst character.

" When ? "

" In the afternoon, talking to the dead man— plotting mischief together."

That was all I could get out of him. Plainly

enough he knew more. But I could not persuade him to tell me.

The night after we made the coast, there was
a full moon, and the man on the lookout put his
trust in the light and went to sleep. It was my
watch, but the spread of canvas kept me from
seeing out. About midnight there came a sudden crash, followed by loud cries of alarm. We
had run into a small sail-boat, and it had filled
and sunk. The ship was rounded to at once,
and a boat was lowered, and I went back in it to
where we could see the men who had been in the
sail-boat, now struggling in the water. The crew
gave way sturdily, but the distance was too great.
One of the men threw up his hands and sank
for the last time, long before we could reach him.
The other had a stronger will and more resistance. There was a high sea, stirred up by the
gale which had blown their boat off shore, and
the waves were fast overcoming the survivor.
As we came near him, he sank. We waited on
our oars in the hope that he would rise, and our
hopes were justified. He came to the surface
within an oar's length of me, but with the life
almost beaten out of him. The men backed
the boat, and I reached out to drag him out of the
water. As he clasped my hand convulsively the
moonlight fell full on our faces. He knew me,
and I knew him; he was the man who had
drugged me and sold me as a sailor; he was the

man who had tried to shoot me; he was the one
enemy I had in the world, though I had saved
his life once, and though I had spared it again.
How he came to be there I did not know, but
I recognized him beyond a doubt, and I saw the
black heart burn on his bare forehead. And he
recognized me; he gave me a look of hatred, as
he said " Not again!" and with a sudden wrench,
he released his hand from mine, threw it above
his head and sank!

We waited, resting on our oars, but he did
not rise again. I had met Constantine Vollonides for the last time!

The next morning the Maltese came to me.

" You tried to save a man's life last night," he
said.

" Yes," I answered, " but the man was
drowned."

" Paolo tells me," he continued,—Paolo was
the name of a sailor in my watch, who had been
in the boat with me the night before,—" that the
man drowned himself. 'Tis well. He was a bad
man. He is better dead."

" Did you know him?" I asked, in astonishment.

" No," he replied; " Paolo was with me in New
York when your enemy talked to the dead mate.
Paolo saw the man last night. It is the same
man. Your enemy is dead. It is well."

" He was my enemy," I said, " and he is dead."

The Maltese lingered by me as though he had something more to say. I had a presentiment that he would tell me now what he had refused to tell me before.

He came closer to me and lowered his voice. " Did you ever hear of the Brotherhood of the Sea ? " he asked, in an awed whisper.

Now, in my wanderings along the shores of the Mediterranean I had been told of a secret order of sailors, a sort of marine Carbonari. I had heard more evil than good of the Brotherhood of the Sea, and I had come to look on it as a league of outlaws, half brigands and half pirates. I told the Maltese what I knew.

" True," he said, " they are bad men. The dead mate belonged to the Brotherhood of the Sea. So did your enemy."

" How do you know ? " I asked.

" I know," he answered; " that is enough." Then he paused and gave me a kindly look. " Did it pain you much to make this voyage ? " he asked.

" Did it pain me much ? " I repeated—and then I told him how I had suffered unspeakable torment every hour since I had left New York, not knowing what might befall you.

He listened sympathetically, and said, " If one voyage were bad, two would be worse."

17

"What do you mean?" I cried.

Again he hesitated a little and drew nearer to
me. "You have heard of the Brotherhood of
the Sea—did you ever hear of the way in which
the Brotherhood of the Sea punished a traitor?"

I shook my head.

"He was drugged, as you were. He was
shipped as a sailor, as you were. When he
reached port, he was drugged again and shipped
on another vessel. And so on again and again.
He was never allowed to set foot on land. He
was passed from ship to ship, never knowing
where he was going. His friends would never
hear of him again. He might live forever at
sea, going from ship to ship, and from port to
port."

"Well?" I said.

"Well, that was to be your fate!" he answered.

"I was to be drugged again," I cried; "and
shipped again? I cannot believe it. Even his
devilish malignity would revolt from that."

"Yes," answered the Maltese, gravely. "That
was to be your fate, I know."

"But how?"

"I know. No matter how. There is a member of the Brotherhood on board this boat. No
matter who. He talks to me. I know. The
dead mate talked to him. All was prepared.
They were to get a great price. Your enemy
would be in California, and when you had been

shipped to the Indies, the dead mate was to tell your enemy."

And from this fate, far worse than death, I had been saved only by the wave which swept the mate overboard as we were going through the Straits of Lemaire.

Less than a week after Constantine Vollonides had unclasped his hand from mine, under the moonlight, off the Californian coast, the *Vengeance of God* made the Golden Gate, and ran in between the heads and up to San Francisco. An hour after we had dropped anchor, I telegraphed Uncle Larry to break the news to you. And in another hour I was in the train for New York.

CHAPTER XVI.

AFTER MANY DAYS.

ABOUT the middle of April there came a bright and glorious spring day; a radiant day of royal weather made for poets and lovers. Winifred Marshall stood in the drawing-room of Mrs. Sutton's house with her hat on. She was dressed in a suit of dark blue cloth, which revealed the exquisite curves of her graceful figure. As she fastened her glove, she glanced again at the clock. Laurence Laughton had come in the morning, with a telegram from Frederick Olyphant, announcing his arrival in New York at five that afternoon; and Winifred had at once besought Uncle Larry to take her to meet him. It was not yet four; but she was impatient and her heart beat fast. When the door-bell rang with a gong-like clang, she ran into the hall. But it was not Laurence Laughton. It was Pussy Palmer.

"Oh, Winifred!" cried this vivacious young lady, "I've such news!"

"Yes?" responded Winifred, with her mind miles away.

" What *do* you think? I'm going to be—"

Here Miss Palmer broke off abruptly, having detected her friend's absence of mind.

" Well," said Winifred, after there had been a little silence, " go on ; what is it? "

" Winnie Marshall ! " Pussy replied, reproachfully. " I think it is just horrid of you. Here I come with news, real *important* news, and you go on thinking about something else all the time and don't pay any attention to me at all."

" I beg your pardon, Pussy," Winifred answered, bending forward impulsively and kissing her friend. " I know I was not listening to you. I—I was thinking of something else. Fred will be in New York in an hour!"

" Will he ? " cried the impulsive Miss Palmer, jumping up and clapping her hands. " I'm so glad! Then you can be married the same time I am!"

" Are you engaged ? " Winifred asked.

" Of course I am. That's what I came to tell you. I've got him at last! I couldn't quite make up my mind for a *long* while whether I wanted him or not, and I forbade his speaking to me until we heard from Fred. But now we *have* heard from Fred, and the little man is so much in love with me, that I took pity on him, and I shall be Mrs. Hobson-Cholmondeley.

" He is a good fellow," Winifred said, " and I feel sure he will make you happy."

"I'll make it warm for him, if he doesn't," retorted Miss Palmer, with the supreme confidence of a young lady quite able to take care of herself. She wore a huge black Rembrandt hat which was most becoming to her fair skin and bright hair.

"And when did it happen?" inquired Winifred.

"Only just now. You are the *first* one I've told. We shan't announce it for a week or two yet. I never expected it; at least, not all of a sudden. He went to the Cooking-School with me this afternoon, and I made chicken-croquettes. And as we were going home, he said that those chicken-croquettes were very good, and I agreed, and said that I should be a boss cook, sooner or later. Then he blushed and hesitated, and said he wished he could engage me permanently as his boss cook. And I said, 'Oh, Mr. Hobson-Cholmondeley!' Then he went on and told me that he had loved me for *weeks*, and he felt he couldn't live without me—and without my croquettes, I suppose. He seemed so serious, as if he really meant it. And he has very pretty hair, don't you think so? There's a lovely wave in it right over his forehead. So I had to accept him. He's very short, I know; but then I am short too; we're a pair. If we lose our money, we can go and be midgets in a dime-museum: I shouldn't wonder if it would be lots of fun!"

There was another clang of the door-bell, and Laurence Laughton was ushered into the drawing-room.

"Oh, Uncle Larry," cried Pussy Palmer, " I've *such* news for you. Guess if you can."

" Well, I don't know," said Uncle Larry, "perhaps you are going to be married ? "

"Somebody must have told you l" Pussy declared, in a disappointed tone.

"And who is the victim ? " asked Laughton, smiling.

" It's Mr. Hobson-Cholmondeley."

" I thought it was to be a secret," interrupted Winifred.

"So it is. I'm not going to tell a *soul*," Miss Palmer retorted. " I don't mind you, Uncle Larry. You don't count ! "

"No, I don't count now," echoed Laurence, sadly.

Winifred looked up at him and caught his weary expression, the only visible sign of the severe struggle for self-mastery. She came up to him, with one of her impulsive movements, and seized his hand, and said.

" My best friend,—how can I ever thank you enough for all the comfort and strength you have given me ? "

" By saying nothing more about it," he answered, raising her hand gently to his lips. Winifred gave him a long and earnest look ; and it may be that she had then her first intimation of the truth.

" And now we must hurry along lively," said Laurence, " if we want to see Fred's arrival."

" I'll skip along," Pussy Palmer remarked; " I've got to walk down to Washington Square, to see the Duchess."

" You have a secret to tell her, too, I suppose," Laurence suggested, as they passed out of the house.

" That's real mean of you," laughed Pussy ; " but, of course, I may give her a hint or two. She is such a *dear* old soul."

Laurence could not help wondering how Mrs. Martin would look if she could have heard herself called, " a dear old soul." He raised his hat as Pussy turned down the Avenue, after she had three times embraced Winifred with exuberant affection.

When Winifred Marshall and Laurence Laughton arrived at the Grand Central Depot, it lacked but a few minutes of five, but the Pacific Express was nearly half an hour behind time. They walked impatiently up and down the long platform, absorbed in their own thoughts, and exchanging only an occasional word. Laughton was in no mood for perfunctory conversation, and Winifred was too happy not to remain silent willingly.

At last the train came in sight; the locomotive darted ahead, and was switched off on a side track without the building, while the cars, impelled by their acquired momentum, rolled forward of their own accord to their appointed place. On the front platform of the foremost car stood Frederick Olyphant, peering ahead eagerly. Before the train stopped he sprang off and clasped Winifred in his arms. She fell upon his neck, sobbing with the relief of joyous excitement. The throng of belated passengers pushed by them, every man intent on his own business, and scarcely deigning to give a glance to this meeting of lovers after a long parting.

"My darling," said Fred, as he kissed her forehead and soothed her with his strong hands.

"Oh, Fred! Fred! you have come back to me at last! I have waited so long—so very long," she said, trying to control herself.

"I will get you a carriage," said Laurence, after he and Fred had exchanged a silent grasp of the hand.

Laughton put them into the carriage and closed the door.

"You are coming with us, Uncle Larry?" urged Winifred, her eyes still wet with tears.

"I will leave you two alone, now," Laurence answered; "I have just remembered that there is a man at the Windsor Hotel whom I ought to see before he goes away."

She understood him then.

"You will dine with me to-night, Uncle Larry," said Fred. "I will call for you."

As the carriage drove on, Winifred gazed at her lover. "How strong and well you look, Fred, and how beautifully brown you are."

Fred took her by the shoulders gently, and turned her toward him and held her at arm's length, while he examined her. "You have suffered, Winifred, my darling; I can see it in your face. But you are more beautiful than ever!"

She let her head fall upon his breast, and said, in a low and trembling voice, "Have you forgiven me, Fred?"

"Forgiven you for what, my darling?" asked he.

"For the wicked way I treated you the day we parted?"

His only answer was another silent kiss.

"You may forgive me," she went on, "for you are so noble and good; but I can never forgive myself."

There was another little space of silence.

Words could not express the happiness Olyphant felt. He accepted the few short minutes of this first meeting with Winifred as a full compensation for the long months of loneliness and misery.

"Do you remember," she said, at last, just

before the carriage stopped. " Do you remember my lending you my ring?"

" The opal? Oh yes,—but it was stolen from me."

" I have it," she returned; " I have put it away for ever. It brought us ill luck, as it brought my mother ill luck, and it shall never be worn again. But your cat's-eye is lucky. I found that, and I have worn it ever since, and at last it has brought me luck—for it has brought you back to me!"

He kissed her again as the carriage drew up before Mrs. Sutton's door.

The wedding took place a month later, about the middle of May. It was as quiet as a wedding can well be. There were not more than twenty present. Among them were Mr. and Mrs. Martin, Mr. and Mrs. Delancey Jones, Miss Pussy Palmer, and Mr. Hobson-Cholmondeley, whose wedding was to take place early in the fall; and, of course, Mr. and Mrs. Sutton, in whose house the ceremony was held. Winifred had insisted on being married in the Lover's Retreat, the little Bower at the end of Mrs. Sutton's dining-room. It was there, she said, that she had so cruelly wronged Fred, and it was there that they had parted, and there she wished to be married. The Lover's Retreat was therefore decked with the fresh flowers of spring. It was just large enough to contain the contracting parties, with the clergyman, Judge Gillespie, who was to give away the bride, and Laurence Laughton, who was the best man. The bride looked surpassingly beautiful in her white silk and creamy lace, and with the orange-blossoms in her hair. The flowers she carried in her hand were not white, as custom rules: she bore a bunch of yellow roses which he had sent her.

THE END.

BRIEF LIST OF BOOKS OF FICTION

PUBLISHED BY CHARLES SCRIBNER'S SONS

George W. Cable.

THE GRANDISSIMES. *New edition.* 12mo, . .	$1.25
OLD CREOLE DAYS. *New edition.* 12mo, . . .	1.25
The same in two parts. 16mo. Cloth, each, 75c.; paper,	
each, ...	.30
MADAME DELPHINE. 12mo, ...	.75

Edward Eggleston.

ROXY. A Tale of Indiana Life. Illustrated. 12mo,	1.50
THE CIRCUIT RIDER. A Tale. Illustrated. 12mo,	1.50
THE HOOSIER SCHOOLMASTER. Illustrated. 12mo,	1.25
THE MYSTERY OF METROPOLISVILLE. Illustrated. 12mo, ...	1.50
THE END OF THE WORLD. A Love Story. Illustrated. 12mo, ...	1.50
Complete Sets (in box), ...	7.25

J. G. Holland.

SEVENOAKS. Small 12mo, . . .	1.25
THE BAY PATH. Small 12mo, . . .	1.25
ARTHUR BONNICASTLE. Small 12mo, . . .	1.25
MISS GILBERT'S CAREER. Small 12mo, . .	1.25
NICHOLAS MINTURN. Small 12mo, . .	1.25

Frances Hodgson Burnett.

THAT LASS O' LOWRIE'S. Illustrated. 12mo. Paper, 50c.; cloth, ...	1.50
HAWORTH'S. Illustrated. 12mo, . . .	1.50
LOUISIANA. 12mo, ...	1.00
SURLY TIM and Other Stories. Small 12mo, . .	1.25

EARLIER STORIES.

LINDSAY'S LUCK. 16mo. Paper, ...	.30
PRETTY POLLY PEMBERTON. 16mo. Paper, . . .	.40
KATHLEEN. 16mo. Paper, ...	.40
THEO. 16mo. Paper, ...	.30
MISS CRESPIGNY. 16mo. Paper, ...	.30

Frank R. Stockton.

RUDDER GRANGE. 12mo. Paper, 60 cents; cloth, $1.25
THE LADY OR THE TIGER? and Other Stories. 12mo.
Paper, 50 cents; cloth, ...   1.00

George P. Lathrop.

NEWPORT. 12mo. Paper, 50c.; cloth, . . .   1.25
AN ECHO OF PASSION. 12mo. Paper, 50c.; cloth,   1.00
IN THE DISTANCE. 12mo. Paper, 50c.; cloth, .   1.00

Saxe Holm's Stories.

FIRST SERIES.

"Draxy Miller's Dowry," "The Elder's Wife," "Whose Wife Was She?" "The One-Legged Dancers," "How One Woman Kept Her Husband," "Esther Wynn's Love Letters." 12mo, Paper, 50c.; cloth, . .   1.00

SECOND SERIES.

"A Four-Leaved Clover," "Farmer Bassett's Romance," "My Tourmaline," "Joe Hale's Red Stocking." "Susan Lawton's Escape." 12mo, Paper, 50c.; cloth, .   1.00

H. H. Boyesen.

FALCONBERG. Illustrated. 12mo, ...   1.50
GUNNAR. A Tale of Norse Life. Square 12mo, .   1.25
TALES FROM TWO HEMISPHERES. Square 12mo, .   1.00
ILKA ON THE HILL TOP, and Other Stories. Square 12mo, 1.00
QUEEN TITANIA. Square 12mo, ...   1.00

Edward Everett Hale.

PHILIP NOLAN'S FRIENDS. Illustrated. 12mo, .   1.75

Augustus M. Swift.

CUPID, M.D. A Story. 16mo, ...   1.00

Howard Pyle.

WITHIN THE CAPES. One vol. 12mo, . . . $1.00

E. T. W. Hoffmann.

WEIRD TALES. 2 vols. 12mo. With portrait, . 3.00

Erckmann-Chatrian Series.

FRIEND FRITZ. 16mo, ... 1.25
THE CONSCRIPT. Illustrated. 16mo, . . . 1.25
WATERLOO. Illustrated. 12mo, ... 1.25
MADAME THERESE. Illustrated 16mo, . . . 1.25
THE BLOCKADE OF PHALSBURG. Illustrated. 16mo, 1.25
THE INVASION OF FRANCE IN 1814. Illustrated. 16mo, 1.25
A MILLER'S STORY OF THE WAR. 16mo, . . 1.25

Jules Verne.

GODFREY MORGAN. Illustrated. 8vo, ... 2 00
MICHAEL STROGOFF. Illustrated. *New edition.* 8vo, . 2.00
A FLOATING CITY, and THE BLOCKADE RUNNERS.
   Illustrated. 8vo, ... 2.00
HECTOR SERVADAC. Illustrated. 8vo, ... 2.00
DICK SANDS. Illustrated. 8vo, ... 3.00
A JOURNEY TO THE CENTRE OF THE EARTH. Illustra-
   ted. 8vo, ... 3.00
THE MYSTERIOUS ISLAND. Illustrated. 8vo, . . 3.00
FROM THE EARTH TO THE MOON DIRECT IN NINETY-
   SEVEN HOURS, TWENTY MINUTES. Illustrated. 12mo, 1.50
STORIES OF ADVENTURE. Comprising " Meridiana," and
   "A Journey to the Centre of the Earth." Illus. 12mo, 1.50
THE DEMON OF CAWNPORE. (Part I of the Steam
   House). Illustrated. 12mo, ... 1.50
TIGERS AND TRAITORS. (Part II of the Steam House).
   Illustrated. 12mo, ... 1.50
EIGHT HUNDRED LEAGUES ON THE AMAZON. (Part I
   of the Giant Raft). Illustrated. 12mo. . . 1.50
THE CRYPTOGRAM. (Part II of the Giant Raft). Illus-
   trated. 12mo, ... 1.50

SCRIBNER'S LIST OF BOOKS OF FICTION.

The King's Men.
A Tale of To-morrow. By Robert Grant, John Boyle O'Reilly, J. S. of Dale, and John T. Wheelwright. 12mo, $1.25

Virginia W. Johnson.
THE FAINALLS OF TIPTON. 12mo, . . . 1.25

Mrs. E. Prentiss.
FRED, MARIA, AND ME. With illustrations. 12mo. *New edition,* 1.00

J. S. of Dale.
GUERNDALE. An Old Story. 12mo. Paper, 50 cents; cloth, ... 1.25
THE CRIME OF HENRY VANE. By the author of " Guerndale." 12mo, ... 1.00

Mary Adams.
AN HONORABLE SURRENDER. 16mo, . . . 1.00

Count Leo Tolstoy.
THE COSSACKS. 12mo, ... 1.25

Donald G. Mitchell.
DR. JOHNS. 12mo. *New edition,* . . . 1.25

Julia Schayer.
TIGER LILY and Other Stories. 12mo, . . . 1.00

Mary Mapes Dodge.
THEOPHILUS AND OTHERS. 12mo, . . . 1.50

A. Perry.
THE SCHOOLMASTER'S TRIAL. 12mo, . . . 1.00

H. C. Bunner and Brander Matthews.
IN PARTNERSHIP. Studies in Story-Telling. 12mo, 1.00

Across the Chasm.
One vol. 12mo, ... 1.00

SCRIBNER'S LIST OF BOOKS OF FICTION.

Stories by American Authors.

A collection of the most noteworthy stories written in recent years, not hitherto printed in book form, now published by arrangement with the authors.

I.—Who Was She? Bayard Taylor. The Documents in the Case, Brander Matthews and H. C. Bunner. One of the Thirty Pieces, William Henry Bishop. Balacchi Brothers, Rebecca Harding Davis. An Operation in Money, Albert Webster. 16mo, ... $ .50

II.—The Transferred Ghost, Frank R. Stockton. A Martyr to Science, Mary Putnam Jacobi, M.D. Mrs. Knollys, J. S. of Dale. A Dinner Party, John Eddy. The Mount of Sorrow, Harriet Prescott Spofford. Sister Silvia, Mary Agnes Tinker. 16mo, ...50

III.—The Spider's Eye, Lucretia P. Hale. A Story of the Latin Quarter, Frances Hodgson Burnett. Two Purse-Companions, George Parsons Lathrop. Poor Ogla-Moga, David D. Lloyd. A Memorable Murder, Celia Thaxter. Venetian Glass, Brander Matthews. 16mo, . .50

IV.—Miss Grief, Constance Fenimore Woolson. Love in Old Cloathes, H. C. Bunner. Two Buckets in a Well, N. P. Willis. Friend Barton's Concern, Mary Hallock Foote. An Inspired Lobbyist, J. W. DeForest. Lost in the Fog, Noah Brooks. 16mo, ...50

V.—A Light Man, Henry James. Yatil, F. D. Millet. The End of New York, Park Benjamin. Why Thomas Was Discharged, George Arnold. The Tachypomp, E. P. Mitchell. 16mo, ...50

VI.—The Village Convict, C. H. White. The Denver Express, A. A. Hayes. The Misfortunes of Bro' Thomas Wheatley, Lina Redwood Fairfax. The Heartbreak Cameo, Mrs. L. W. Champney. Miss Eunice's Glove, Albert Webster. Brother Sebastian's Friendship, Harold Frederic. 16mo, ...50

VII.—The Bishop's Vagabond, Octave Thanet. Lost, Edward Bellamy. Kirby's Coals of Fire, Louise Stockton. Passages from the Journal of a Social Wreck, Margaret Floyd. Stella Grayland, James T. McKay. The Image of San Donato, Virginia W. Johnson, . .50

VIII.—The Brigade Commander, J. W. DeForest. Split Zephyr, Henry A. Beers. Zerviah Hope, Elizabeth Stuart Phelps. The Life Magnet, Alvey A. Adee. Osgood's Predicament, Elizabeth D. B. Stoddard, . .50

IX.—Marse Chan, Thomas Nelson Page. Mr. Bixby's Christmas Visitor, Charles S. Gage. Eli, C. H. White. Young Strong of the Clarion, Millicent Washburn Shinn. How Old Wiggins Wore Ship, Captain Rowland F. Coffin. "—— Mas Has Come," Leonard Kipp, . . .50

X.—Pancha, T. A. Janvier. The Ablest Man in the World, F. P. Mitchell. Young Moll's Peevy, C. A. Stephens. Manmat'ha, Charles de Kay. A Daring Fiction, H. H. Boyesen. The Story of Two Lives, Julia Schayer, ...50

Complete Sets, 10 vols. in a box, $5.00.

www.ingramcontent.com/pod-product-compliance
Lightning Source LLC
Chambersburg PA
CBHW060610030726
47498CB00005B/1625